Copyright © 2022 E S Monk

Published 2022

ISBN 9798826110249

Pine Tree Meadows

By

E.S. Monk

For

Nana Joan

Phoebe

Phoebe clenched her eyes shut as she felt the warm liquid soaking through her shirt.

"You have got to be kidding me," she mumbled under her breath as she tentatively peeked out of one eye and saw several pairs of shoes heading in her direction, including an immaculate pair of four-inch patent leather black stilettos. "Absolutely bloody perfect."

She found herself splayed out like a plump seal basking in the sun, on the very public office floor. *Only I could trip up over my own feet in flat ballet pumps,* Phoebe shamefully thought.

Then the cackling reached her ears from Miss Stilettos. "That must be Mr Parker's new personal assistant, what does she look like!" she announced to the crowd of concerned observers before promptly stepping over her and barking, "Back to work, all of you."

Cringing inwardly with mortification and knowing that she would have to face the unfortunate mess she had managed to get herself into, she patiently watched the assortment of shoes scurry off, before slowly sitting herself up to survey the damage of her brand new pristine white shirt. *Well, there's no recovering from that,* she thought dismally, looking down at her drenched, coffee-stained shirt. *What an entrance for my first day!*

She felt a shadow fall over her, followed by the words, "Oh my, are you ok?"

Looking up, she was met with sparkling green eyes on a friendly, concerned-looking face.

"Here, let me help you up," said Green Eyes. "I'm Jack."

She felt Jack slip his arms around her and haul her to her feet. "Thank you, I'm

Phoebe, it's my first day," she explained. "I was supposed to deliver the coffee to Mr Parker before his morning meeting, but, well things haven't quite gone according to plan," she replied miserably.

He nodded in reply, acknowledging her predicament. "I'm afraid I can't help with the coffee situation, but you might be in luck with the shirt," said Jack. "I'm meeting friends after work so I happen to have a clean shirt with me today if you would like to borrow it?" he continued, as he rummaged around in his backpack before pulling out a navy blue and white pin stripped shirt and offering it to her.

Phoebe looked up at the tall, broad man towering over her, quickly weighing up her options of her stained shirt or oversized clean shirt before facing her new boss without the required coffee.

"Thank you, that's really kind of you," she replied, graciously accepting his shirt.

Hurrying off to the Ladies, she locked herself into a small cubicle to change. She heard the door swing open, followed by haughty cackling.

"Did you see the state of the new PA? Could she be any more of a disaster? And chubby with it!" Phoebe could feel her cheeks burning with embarrassment, and she recognised the voice as Miss Stilettos.

"And what is she wearing? I wouldn't be caught dead in that outdated navy blue skirt. She clearly has zero fashion sense!" her companion laughed, before they both left the restroom in a cloud of expensive perfume.

Phoebe closed her eyes and tried to hold back the tears. *Today is turning out to be a very bad day,* she thought, fumbling to do up the buttons of Jack's shirt with her shaking hands. It smelt clean, with a hint of masculinity to it. *Such an intimate thing to wear a stranger's clothes,* she mused. *I'll make sure I do something kind for him in return.*

Attempting to give the large shirt some shape, she tied it in a knot at her waist, then tentatively peeked around the cubicle door, just to double check her taunters had left. Alone in the privacy of the ladies' room, she looked in the mirror. *Oh dear,* she thought, *that will not do.* She hastily ran her fingers through her hair before running the tap and splashing cool water on her tear-stained face. *I need to make a good impression when I see Mr Parker.*

"Don't let one faux pas ruin this for you," she told herself in the mirror. And with a determined nod, she slung her handbag over her shoulder and with as much confidence as she could muster, opened the door, and marched purposefully across the office floor.

"Ah, Phoebe, there you are," said Mr Parker. Phoebe's heart sank into her ballet pumps when she saw Miss Stilettos standing beside him, smirking at her. "I wanted to introduce you to Laura, my advertising and marketing manager. Laura and I work closely together so you two will probably be seeing a lot of each other," he said, smiling from one woman to the other, clearly not noticing the frosty glare Laura was unleashing on Phoebe.

The look had not been lost on Phoebe, however. The gazelle-like creature before her sported poker straight blonde hair cropped in a sleek bob, and a long-sleeved, knee-length, body-hugging black dress adorned her size six figure. She looked like she had just stepped off the front cover of Vogue and both she and Phoebe knew, in that moment, that Phoebe was without a doubt, to be found wanting when it came to glamour and fashion, and Laura held her in complete disdain for her ignorance. Phoebe offered out her hand, praying that it wasn't clammy, and looked down at the immaculately manicured hand that grasped hers just that little bit too firmly to be a friendly greeting, and Laura's steely blue eyes glared down at her.

"Wonderful that you two have met," said the enthusiastic Mr Parker. "Come along now Phoebe, let's get you settled at your desk."

Mr Parker was proving to be a kind boss. He was efficient and a firm believer in hard work, with high expectations that his employees follow the same principles, but he was also down to earth, thoughtful, and believed if he was kind to his staff, they would work hard and be loyal to him in return. It took many hands to run his Affordable Homes architectural business and with the workload constantly streaming in, he needed the right team to keep it running like clockwork.

Laura, on the other hand, was as prickly as a hedgehog and about as helpful as a chocolate tea pot. She had given Phoebe the wrong files to photocopy for Mr Parkers morning meeting, deliberately, judging by the smug look she gave Phoebe when Mr Parker gruffly complained, in front of everyone, before sending her off to photocopy then distribute the correct details to the potential clients. Mr Parker seemed disappointed by having his important meeting delayed by twenty minutes. *And quite rightly,* Phoebe admitted to herself.

Phoebe, sitting at her desk, held her head in her hands and sighed. As far as first days went, this had to be one of the worst she had ever encountered. She had been so excited about starting her new job in the city of Truro. A true country girl at heart, her previous employment had been in the small local town next to her home, situated in a little village near the beautiful Cornish moors. It was a friendly village, the sort where everyone knew everyone and always looked out for one another. Her receptionist's job at a small hotel was something she loved but the meagre pay was not enough to fund her new venture, and so she had needed to seek work further afield. The half an hour's commute was well worth it to be earning almost twice as much money, and she needed the cash for her and Penelope. She had even swallowed her pride and moved back in with her mum to help save even more pennies. *I will not let Miss Stilettos ruin this for me,* she thought determinedly.

She jolted and pinged her eyes open when she felt a hand on her shoulder.

"Sorry! I didn't mean to startle you," laughed Jack, his green eyes twinkling at her. "I heard about the meeting. Don't worry too much, these things happen."

Phoebe looked away from him, embarrassed that he knew about her morning's mix up.

"We all make mistakes, Mr Parker will have forgotten all about it by tomorrow," he said kindly.

Phoebe looked up and met his eyes, "Thank you, it's been a bit of a tough first day," she said with a wry smile.

Joel

Joel reached down and ran his fingers through Eliza's silky mane.

"Our favourite view isn't it, girl?" he said to his horse as they stood quietly, all alone, at the edge of the woodland track. In one direction, a patchwork quilt of fields stretched as far as their eyes could see under a clear blue sky, and when they turned around, there were miles and miles of treetops, and they could hear the leaves rustling in the gentle breeze, enticing them into the forest for an exhilarating ride, to gallop along the narrow tracks and jump any fallen down trees in their wake.

Joel directed Eliza down the steep track, weaving between the trees, a route Eliza could have done on her own, she knew it so well. They had been galloping these woods for near on fifteen years, and they never tired of it. There was always a new track to find, a different part of the river to cross, and new logs to jump, and for the most part, Joel gave Eliza a free reign to decide the path she wanted to take. He held more trust in her than any other living creature he knew.

The path evened out and he asked Eliza to move into a steady trot. That was her cue, and from then on, she would make the decisions when to transition smoothly between trot, canter, and gallop, depending on the surface beneath her, and Joel just went along for the ride. He could feel her picking up the pace, the wind whistling between the trees, and they were ff.

Cantering effortlessly along the narrow track, listening to the familiar beat of Eliza's hooves beneath him, Joel cast his mind back to the day their lifelong partnership began. On the morning of his twenty-first birthday, after enjoying the routine special birthday breakfast of bacon and eggs, followed by his mother's legendary homemade cinnamon buns, his mum and dad had sent secretive smiles between themselves and announced his birthday present was not actually at home. Joel, wondering what on earth his parents were up to, climbed enthusiastically into the back of his dad's car.

Ten minutes later, they pulled up outside a livery yard, and Joel felt excitement bubble up in him as to what the destination might mean. His parents hovered anxiously on the yard as they all waited for the owner to meet them. Joel's parents were not 'horsey', but once they realised the passion Joel held for them, they did everything in their power to ensure his passion was encouraged and allowed to flourish. However, buying and owning a horse had been an expense they couldn't meet, especially as they were supporting him during his farriery apprenticeship, so Joel was struggling to understand why they were standing on a horse yard.

"Hello," called out Tommy, the yard owner. "This way, follow me."

Joel followed his parents and Tommy across the yard and down an aisle between the stables.

Tommy stood back and pointed inside the stable, joining in the secretive smiles with Joel's parents. "In there!"

"She's yours," smiled his mum.

Joel could contain his curiosity no more. Striding over to the stable door, he peered in, and there she was, nestled in a warm cosy straw bed, his beautiful Eliza. On seeing him, she staggered up on her oversized baby legs and looked at him with her soft, large brown eyes, and Joel was absolutely smitten.

"She's the right type, isn't she?" questioned his dad. "The Irish one?"

"And the colour? She's the right colour, this is the one you said is your favourite?" asked his mum, concern etched on her face. Clearly, she wasn't quite convinced that the blackfilly would indeed transform into a dapple-grey mare.

Joel's heart melted at the effort and kindness his parents had showered on him, giving him this perfect horse. He worried how they could have possibly afforded her.

"We're sorry she's only a baby, but she's a pedigree Irish draft though," his father announced proudly, passing him her paperwork. "But I'm sorry son, we just couldn't stretch to a fully-grown one, all ready to go." It was as if his father had read his mind about the money and wanted to assure him that they hadn't blown every penny they had on this horse for him.

"But we thought at least this way, you'll have her right from the beginning, really make her your own horse," his mum stammered, looking at him with wide eyes.

"She's absolutely perfect in every way," he enthused, trying to contain the emotion in his voice as he opened his arms and reached out to embrace both of his parents. The last thing he wanted was for them to think he was disappointed because she was a foal. Far from it.

"We can manage with half of your wages," his mum whispered, "so you can afford her upkeep."

On that day, Joel had been completely bowled over with the generosity of his hard-working parents, and the realisation that they would have gone without for goodness knows how long in order to save enough money for him to have the precious filly. He had made a mental note to himself - *as soon as I'm a qualified farrier and earning decent money, they will want for nothing.*

"Nineteen years ago, to the day," he told his horse, enjoying the memory, then he laughed out loud as he remembered the look on Phoebe's face, when she had found out that her treat to stay the night at a friend's house had not really been a treat for her at all. It had been strategically organised so that Joel could enjoy the moment with his parents, just the three of them, with his little sister out of the way. She had been absolutely furious! And exclaimed that she wanted a pony too.

Her parents placated her by telling her she could have her own horse when she turned twenty-one, which led to more wails of how unfair her life was with six long years to wait. She had sulked for an entire week.

"I only wish Dad was here to see what a wonderful horse you turned out to be, girl," Joel said, with a heavy sadness in his voice.

It never failed to amaze him, how his non-horsey mum and dad had miraculously chosen the most perfect horse for him to share his life with. He couldn't possibly imagine his life without her now. She had been his ever-faithful friend and loyal partner for nineteen years, and a constant reminder of what his loving parents had done for him.

Alone in the woods, with only Eliza for company, he felt a closeness to his father, the man who had always nurtured and supported his love of horses in every way that he could. And amongst the rustling pine trees and tweeting birds, he felt contentment in himself that the financial sacrifices his father had made over the years had not been wasted. His love of horses had never wavered and he now ran his own successful farrier business. He hoped his dad would be proud of him, with all that he had managed to achieve thanks to the support and encouragement his parents had given him.

Bridget

Bridget placed the food bowl on the floor and watched William greedily gobble it up. She laughed quietly to herself. It never failed to amuse her that a male, of any species, was governed by their stomach!

Her son, Joel, was always a pleasure to cook for. He often popped over for his evening meal and cleared his plate with gusto, and always had room for one of her homemade puddings.

However, her little William, a miniature chestnut Shetland, with a luxurious flaxen mane and tail, was by far the greediest of them all. For a creature of such small stature, he could happily eat his way through his own body weight of food if he was allowed too. His portly tum was a constant worry of hers and she meticulously weighed his daily feed in order to provide enough nutrients and minerals without adding any excess weight.

Once the slurping and furious licking came to an end, she prized the bowl off William, tossed it over the stable door, slipped his teeny head collar on and set about his morning pamper session. Aside from eating, William's second favourite thing in life was to be adored and he would stand for hours to be groomed and fussed by Bridget. And she was happy to oblige. Since losing her beloved husband twelve years ago, and with Joel and Phoebe grown up and living their own lives, her life as a devoted wife and mother had crumbled down around her, leaving her feeling both hopelessly alone and terrifyingly not needed. For Bridget, there was nothing worse than not feeling needed in this world. She had enjoyed every moment of her married life and to lose her husband, the man she was supposed to share her whole life with, when she was only forty-five had left her heartbroken and empty. And then William came into her life.

Bridget didn't know anything about horses, nor had much of an interest in them, until Joel became obsessed with them, and Phoebe swiftly followed in his footsteps. And like any mother would, she took an interest in order to support her children. Always from the side-lines, mind, and still to this day she had never actually sat on one.

It had been the first Christmas after Jacob died that William had come into her life. Christmas was Jacob's favourite time of year; their household was always brimming with festive merriment and his excitement was infectious. The tree decorating was a family affair, and even when the children became adults, they always chose to spend Christmas with their parents. The house was adorned with decorations, and Bridget's kitchen was at the heart of the festivities as she cooked and baked the family's favourite Christmas treats throughout the holiday period. The thought of the first Christmas without Jacob had filled her with dread. Once the Christmas music started on the radio, and the shops burst into the Christmas spirit, with beautiful window displays and wonderful gifts on sale - the gifts she and Jacob would have chosen together for family and friends - her heart ached, and the shroud of grief and depression engulfed her.

Joel and Phoebe had come over on Christmas Eve, just like they always did, and she had half-heartedly cooked the evening meal, as if she was on auto pilot. Her brain knew what to do after all her years spent in the kitchen, but her mind was miles away. Her heart was empty of merriment and filled to the brim with grief.

Christmas morning arrived bright and early. Phoebe and Joel had to sort the horses before they could relax and enjoy their day off. Bridget didn't want to get out of bed. She simply couldn't face the day without Jacob. Phoebe had crept into her bedroom at six, slipped under the covers and placed her arm around her.

"It's time to get up, Mum," she had whispered. "I can't go to the yard without you. Dad would always come on Christmas morning; he'd add carrots and apples to the horses' feed. He always said that it was Christmas for them too, and they deserved a treat. I can't face going without you."

That was the moment when Bridget felt ashamed. She had been so wrapped up in her own grief that she had not been there to support her children. They had lost their father and they needed her now more than ever. Hauling herself out of bed, she and Phoebe found Joel waiting in the kitchen.

Joel held his arms out and embraced her in a welcoming hug. "Merry Christmas, Mum," he mumbled, and she could hear the thickness in his voice, and his attempt to hide his own grief in order to support her and Phoebe. But she was his mother, and he could not hide it from her.

"Merry Christmas sweetheart," she replied, and beckoned Phoebe to join them in their embrace. Holding Phoebe and Joel in her arms, for the first time since Jacob's death, she felt a surge of gratitude in her heart. She still had her children, her wonderful children. From now on, she would be there for them.

"Let's go and feed the horses," she announced. The three of them, wrapped up against the wintery weather, piled into Joel's pick-up truck and made the ten-minuet journey to the livery yard.

She followed them into the feed room, producing carrots and apples from her pockets. "They deserve a Christmas treat, too," she said, and she saw tentative smiles break out on Phoebe and Joel's faces.

After bustling around in the feed room, Joel and Phoebe picked up their respective feed bowls, and then handed her a much smaller bowl with a chopped carrot and apple in it. She looked up at them questioningly.

"For the new addition to our herd!" Phoebe exclaimed. "Come on, Mum, the horses are hungry."

Dutifully carrying the little bucket, she followed her children on to the yard. She saw Eliza and Penelope's beautiful faces, waiting expectantly, as they poked their heads over their stable door. She looked at the third stable. It seemed empty, with no inquisitive head peeking over that door*What are they on* *about? What new addition?*

She jumped when a loud bang erupted from the seemingly empty stable. And then another, and another.

"I think someone is hungry!" Joel grinned at his mother.

Curiosity finally got the better of her, and, following Joel's lead, she slowly made her way to the third stable and tentatively looked inside. And there he was, the beautiful, teeny tiny William.

"Oh my word," she gushed. "What an adorable baby. He's so small! So much smaller than Eliza and Penelope when they arrived."

Phoebe laughed. "Mum, he's not a baby! He's a miniature Shetland and he's fully grown. That's it," she giggled, "that's as big as he will get."

Bridget then laughed along with her daughter at her horsey ignorance. "But if he won't be getting any bigger, what will you do with him? Even I know that he's too small to ride!"

"He's not for us," Joel quietly explained. "We have our horses. He's for you. We thought it would be a way for you to be more involved. Dad loved spending time with the horses, and over the years he learned so much about them, and he always told us that he enjoyed being a part of our horsey world. We thought you might like to take part in it too? And..."

Bridget watched Joel and Phoebe glance at each other, and they both shifted uncomfortably in their wellington boots.

"And what?" she replied quietly.

"And we thought William would be a reason for you to get out of the house," admitted Phoebe. "He's super friendly, and really safe. Joel and I spent ages picking out the right one for you."

Bridget felt her heart swell with pride at how thoughtful and kind her children were, and she acknowledged how desperate they were for her to step up and take their father's place in their private world of horses. She looked down at the little ginger fluff ball, and as if feeling her eyes on him, he turned to look at her, and on the tips of his tippy toes, he had reached up and gently snuffled her hand resting on his stable door.

A loud rumble from William's belly brought Bridget back into the present. Giggling to herself, she stood back and admired her handsome, immaculate pony. "Come along then William, it's time for you to go and play with Eliza and Penelope in the paddock, and you can have a nibble at some grass! And I have to get home, I have Joel's fortieth birthday feast to prepare."

Phoebe

Phoebe pulled up to Pine Tree Meadows and smiled. It may look like a ramshackle building site but all she saw was the blossoming potential, and the dream she and Joel held for so long finally turning into a reality.

Pine Tree Meadows had initially comprised of a dilapidated farmhouse, three neglected old barns in disrepair and six acres of land. Now, it consisted of a dilapidated farmhouse, two fallen-down barns, one static caravan and one spanking new yard. It was situated on the other side of the large forest to where she and Joel previously stabled their horses, and being surrounded by fir trees, there was no doubt how the property acquired its name. The riding opportunities it offered were the best in the area. Whatever the weather, there were always keen riders pulling up in the forest's public car park, unloading their horses from horse boxes then enjoying a good canter along the woodland tracks. But for Phoebe and Joel, they had the luxury of riding there every day, or a ten-minute hack along the quiet country lanes brought them to the open moors. It really was riding paradise.

Phoebe and Joel had decided unanimously that the stables should be built first. That way they could move Eliza, Penelope and William and save some money on livery fees. The five stables and spacious tack room, designed meticulously by them both, were the beating heart of the otherwise downtrodden property.

All in good time, Phoebe thought, *Rome was not built in a day!* She climbed out of her car and strolled over to the tack room. Collecting the head collars, she made her way over to the paddocks to bring the horses in for the night.

Penelope was waiting for her, like she always was, as soon as she heard her car trundling along the driveway. Penelope liked her home comforts. *Just like me,* Phoebe mused. She couldn't fathom why Joel would choose to live in a caravan on the building site when he had the opportunity to move back in with their mum, just like she had done, and enjoy the benefits of central heating, hot showers, and her mother's delicious cooking. But he had been adamant. He wanted to be on site to keep an eye on the horses and oversee the building works.

After settling Eliza and William in their stables for the night, Phoebe unlatched Penelope's door and slipped inside. After her hectic first day at work, she needed five minutes to unwind, and taking a few moments to listen to Penelope methodically munching on her hay allowed her to do just that.

Penelope was a bright bay, sixteen hand warmblood mare, and just like Eliza, she had been given to her from her parents on her twenty-first birthday. However, hers and Penelope's journey had been somewhat different to Joel's and Eliza's. During the long six years she'd had to wait for her own horse, her time had been spent watching the partnership of Joel and Eliza develop. He had backed her and trained her himself and made it all look so easy; so easy that Phoebe had come down to earth with a bump, literally, when she and Penelope did not follow the same path.

Joel was what she called a truly gifted horseman, and she had to admit it - she did not hold the same qualities. She loved horses, that was for sure, but her ability and confidence were lacking. Truth be told, when the time came, it was Joel who trained Penelope for her. Joel was the first person to climb aboard Penelope's broad back. Again, he made it look so easy that Phoebe couldn't wait to take over and ride herself, but that first attempt had ended in disaster. Penelope had sensed her lack of confidence and bucked her off. Without the gentle guidance and confidence Joel exuded for the newly backed horse, Penelope suddenly feared the unknown.

Finally, after months of lessons from Joel, she and Penelope began to trust each other and could ride around the makeshift paddock arena together. But when it came to hacking out in the woods, it was like they were back to square one. Joel took over Penelope's training again and taught her how to cope with riding away from the yard and slowly built her confidence for riding into the unknown.

Phoebe had to just sit back and watch, from the safety of reliable Eliza, as Joel expertly trained her horse for her.

Phoebe smiled at her mare. "What a journey we have been on over the years," she said, grateful that she and Penelope had stuck it out and worked hard, together, at their relationship. "We got there in the end, didn't we, girl." She affectionately stroked the horses nose, then gave her a kiss before explaining, "I've got to go now, I promised Mum I'd be on time for Joel's birthday dinner."

As she pushed open the front door to her mum's house, she could smell the delicious feast wafting from the kitchen. She knew immediately what it was. Her mum cooked the same thing every year for Joel's birthday - roast beef with all the trimmings, followed by apple crumble with buckets of custard. Her mouth watered just thinking about it.

"Is that you love?" her mum called out.

"Hi Mum, Hi Joel, I'm home," she replied, kicking off her boots and heading towards the kitchen.

"Perfect timing, I'm just dishing up," said her mum. "Oh my, what on earth are you wearing?" Bridget chuckled when she caught sight of her.

"Why are you wearing one of my shirts? You look ridiculous!" laughed Joel.

Flopping down on a chair at the kitchen table, Phoebe giggled, "It's not yours! You will never believe the day I've had." Tucking into her roast beef, she regaled the disastrous day to her family.

Jack

"Chloe, will you hurry up please, we're going to be late," Jack hollered up the stairs.

"I can't find my silver hoop earrings," came his daughter's response, without any sound of footsteps heading towards him.

"Your life will not end if you don't wear earrings today. Now come on, or you can walk," he replied in frustration.

He heard her clomping down the stairs. *Finally! Honestly,* he thought, *teenage girls are enough to test any man's patience!*

He handed Chloe a warm croissant to eat in the car, as was their morning routine. She spent so long faffing around, doing lord knows what, that she was never down the stairs in time for breakfast.

"Thanks, Dad," said Chloe, tucking straight into the croissant as she sauntered through the front door that he held open for her.

During the ten-minute drive to school, Jack listened to Chloe babble away about the complicated, dramatic lives she and her friends were living. He had learnt over the last three years, since Chloe became a teenager, that it was best only to offer advice when asked. Impromptu parental advice was *so* not needed when you were sixteen. Instead, he listened to her waffle on and did his best to remember the names of her large circle of giggling girlfriends. He forced himself to hold his tongue when boys' names were casually dropped into conversation.

He and Chloe had always enjoyed an easy relationship. They just seemed to get along. He always encouraged her independence, and in order for that to flourish, he had to trust her. She often gave him a daily run down of the events of her life, usually in great detail – it was like one of those soap programmes she and her friends watched. Because she was so open with him, he hoped that meant she really did trust him, and that she would come to him with any problems as and when they might arise. He didn't believe in control and punishment; he knew that relationships were built on mutual trust. She was slowly turning into a young adult, and he must allow her to become one.

Pulling up outside of the school gates, Chloe leaned over to give him a kiss on his cheek. "Bye, Dad," she called, already halfway out of his car, and he watched her stroll over to her group of friends, before turning back for a quick wave, as she always did. Then she headed into school for her first class.

Jack sighed a heavy sigh. *When did she get so big!* He thought of how he used to swing her up onto his shoulders to her shrieks of laughter and great delight. And when did the invitations to her teddy bears' tea parties stop coming? One day she was tiny, then the next, boom, an almost independent teenager. A beeping car brought him back into the present. He put up his hand to signal an apology for holding up the line for the other busy parents needing to drop their children off before heading off to work themselves.

Time I got myself to work, thought Jack, guiding his car through the overcrowded school driveway.

Arriving at work in the nick of time, he smiled and offered the usual polite morning greetings to his co-workers as he swiftly made his way towards his office. As the company's head architect, he was privileged to have his own office, and on entering, he saw a white box, tied up with pink ribbon, in the middle of his desk. On closer inspection, he noticed it was sitting on his now freshly washed and ironed shirt, the one he lent to the new girl yesterday.

He opened the card that was attached to the box.

Thank you so much for saving me on my first day! Hope you enjoy the cupcakes. Phoebe x

Touched by her kind gesture, he carefully undid the pink bow and opened the box. Four vanilla sponge cupcakes, covered with vanilla buttercream, were inside. Each one was decorated with a delicious selection of chocolates on top. His mouth watered at the sight of them, and he couldn't resist eating one immediately.

Brushing the crumbs off himself, he reached towards the cupcake box for another. That new girl really could bake! He slowly peeled the second cupcake out of its case, then took a large bite. Savouring the delicious flavours, he chewed slowly, and cast his eyes out of his window, over the office floor. He spotted her instantly. Laura was towering over her, no doubt berating her, if the aggressive look on her face was anything to go by. He wondered why Laura was so opposed to the new girl. Maybe she felt that Phoebe was competition for Mr Parker's favourite, a position Laura had always held.

He looked at both women. Laura was groomed to perfection and ever the ruthless professional. And then there was Phoebe. He smiled to himself as he watched her. Petite, curvy, and feminine, with her honey blonde hair tied up in a bedraggled ponytail. He sensed a warm glow surrounding her. On a whim, he whipped out his sketch book, the one he kept with him wherever he went for his own private drawings, and grinned. In no time at all he pencilled a large, fierce dragon, easily identifiable as Laura, with the comical, poker straight bob he had etched, breathing fire over a beautiful fairy. The fairy, encircled by a protective force, looked gently up at the dragon, taking no heed of its fury. And the fairy's eyes were filled with innocence and kindness.

After completing his sketch, Jack looked up and noticed that both of his muses had parted, and no doubt gone back to work. He carefully slid his sketch book back into his bag, switched his computer on, and helped himself to a third cupcake whilst skimming his diary for the day's appointments.

Joel

Joel trundled up the drive to Hollybrook stables. A full day's work, and always plenty of friendly people to chat too, plus a constant stream of cups of tea and slices of homemade cake. He always looked forward to his days at Hollybrook.

"Hello Clare," he called out to the owner of Hollybrook stables.

"Hi Joel," she replied, grinning widely. She was sporting a sun-kissed golden tan.

"How was the honeymoon?" Joel asked, as he dropped his tools to the ground and gratefully accepted the cup of tea Clare thrust into his hands.

"Absolutely wonderful," exclaimed Clare. "Barbados truly is paradise!"

Joel listened to Clare chatter away about her amazing honeymoon with her new husband, Matthew, whilst he set about removing Ghost's shoes.

"The beaches were just glorious, and what a thrill to gallop across the sands with the gentle crashing of the waves at your side. And you'll never believe it, on more than one occasion, when we were swimming in the sea, we saw ginormous turtles! They would swim elegantly around us for a few minutes before heading off to go about their turtle business, what an experience!"

Joel stood up and faced Clare, genuinely pleased she'd had a wonderful time, and with a wry smile, he replied, "And now you're back to work!"

"Indeed I am!" she laughed in reply. "I'll go and fetch Sundance and Pipsqueak from the paddock, then they'll be ready for when you've finished Ghost."

After two hours, Joel was now fully caught up and in the loop about the engagement of Joe, Clare's son, to his long-term girlfriend, Riley, and all the excitement and planning that went with it for a spring wedding at Hollybrook. Joel finally sat down for a short break. It was futile to try and refuse Clare. She always insisted that he sit down for fifteen minutes to enjoy his tea and cake in a civilised manner, before the liveries arrived for Joel to shoe their horses. And just on cue, Suzie and Clarissa plodded up the drive.

"Hello Joel," she called out as she waved to him. "I hope we haven't kept you? The weather is so nice today, Clarissa and I thought we'd enjoy a morning ride!"

"Not at all," Joel replied. "I'm ready when you are." Joel liked Suzie, and while he worked, she chatted away ten to the dozen about her large collection of animals, her husband Luke, and her two sons, John and Joseph. She bubbled with positivity and once she'd caught him up to speed on all of her own gossip, the conversation turned to him. And like clockwork, just as he handed Clarissa's lead rope over to her, and he made a start on her little donkey, Mistletoe, she blurted out her regular question.

"So, Joel. Seeing anyone at the moment? Any gossip to report?"

He smiled to himself. He just couldn't help but laugh along with Suzie and the animated tales of her somewhat chaotic, yet contented lifestyle, and her persistent nose for snffing out gossip!

He laughed out loud. "No dating gossip!" he replied, but feeling he should offer her something, he continued. "The building work at Pine Trees is well underway. The stables and yard are complete, Eliza, Penelope and William now live there, and all of the barns have been cleared and gutted."

He was rewarded with her beaming smile. "Fantastic news, Joel."

A car that had just pulled into the driveway diverted their attention.

"Ah, it's Rose!" Suzie exclaimed. "I had better turn my three back out in the paddock to make room for Winter. Have you finished with Gilly?" She gently stroked the huge horse belonging to her husband.

"All done," said Joel, handing over Gilly's lead rope. He felt anticipation build inside him as he watched Rose climb out of her car and head up to the yard. Two months ago, he had spoken to Rose about rescuing a dog, but it had to be the right dog. He was after a dog to keep him company whilst at work, but because he went to so many different yards, it was imperative that he or she have the correct temperament to be around both horses and people. Rose had said that she would keep an eye out for him. She was one of the vets who volunteered at Rosewin, the local rescue centre. Her partner, Andrew, worked for Rosewin, as well as its sister equine charity in Devon. So Rose was very much in the know of any new dogs that came into the centre, but it would take time and he knew he would have to be patient.

"Joel, hello," Rose said in greeting, as she joined him on the yard.

"Afternoon Rose, how's Winter?" he politely asked. He was desperate to enquire about the dog, but it was Winter he was here to see, and he must be professional.

"Perfect, as always!" she laughed, leading her beautiful bay mare out of the stable.

Joel liked Winter. Well, he liked all horses, each and every one of them, but there was something about Winter that reminded him of Eliza. She had the same quiet way about her, and the same gentle, naturally trusting personality. And what a credit to her after the horrific neglect she had endured before Rose rescued her. Winter gently snuffled his hand, and he stroked her nose before getting to work on removing her shoes.

"So, I have news," announced Rose. "But I don't want you to get too excited. She hasn't been signed off to be rehomed yet. She has her final behavioural test next week, and then her final medical check the week after. I've explained to the rescue about you, and they are willing to offer you first refusal once she's ready."

Joel couldn't help but allow himself to feel a bit excited. Rose was far too professional and sensible to divulge this information if she didn't think there was a high possibility that this dog might be the one for him.

"What's her story?" he enquired, as he moved on to remove the next shoe.

"Approximately two years old, and judging by the state her, she's been a stray for the entire time. She was hit by a car three weeks ago and brought in for medical treatment. No collar or chip, or any form of identification. The rescue did the usual call out for anyone that might have lost a dog, but no one has come forward to claim her. She's a dear little thing, not a clue what her breeding is! She's some sort of brindle coloured, wire haired terrier cross breed. So far, her temperament is proving to be kind and gentle, but like I said, the final behavioural assessment is next week. The staff have named her Katie. And there is just something about her, I don't know what it is, maybe a sixth sense or something," she said, with a chuckle. "I just get the feeling she is meant to be yours."

"When can I go and visit her?" asked Joel.

"Whenever you like! Just give them a call to arrange a time, they're expecting you."

"All finished," Joel said, standing up and looking at Rose. "Thank you, I really appreciate your help."

"No problem, any dog would be lucky to have a home with you," Rose said kindly. "I'd better turn Winter out now, I've got a foal castration booked in next! I've got be there in half an hour."

Joel watched her walk away, his mind buzzing at the thought of Katie. His private thoughts did not last long. Two cars trundled down the drive, one behind the other, and pulled up in Hollybrook's carpark. He smiled and waved as his next two customers climbed out of their respective vehicles and hurried onto the yard to greet him.

"Hi Joel," said Jem.

"Sorry I'm late," said Ellen.

"Hello ladies," Joel called out. "Don't worry, no one's late! I've only just finished Winter."

And he was back to work, all thoughts of Katie quelled as he listened to Jem and Ellen fill him in on all their news while he worked quietly and efficiently on their horses, Jupiter and Pandora.

Lilly

Lilly unclipped Sooty's lead, gave him a final stoke, then closed his kennel door. *Who's next,* she thought, pulling her list out of her jeans pocket. *Ah, Rascal!* She walked down the aisle of kennels and stopped outside his door. The little West Highland white terrier bounced up and down in delight on seeing her, knowing it was his turn to go for a walk next. *Rascal by name and rascal by nature,* she giggled to herself, as she let herself into the overly excited dog's kennel.

"Come on then," she said to the little dog, clipping the lead onto his collar. "Let's go for a walk, you need to burn off some energy!"

Lilly loved her job. She had fallen into it quite by accident. Her previous career path had been child minding. After completing her collage course in childcare, she had moved straight into the profession by setting up her own child-minding business from her home in Dorset for twelve years. She had enjoyed her work, especially when her sister, a high-flying businesswoman, entrusted her son Oliver to her. Her sister, Annie, loved and adored Oliver, there was no doubt about it, but she was a career woman at heart and as soon as her maternity leave was up, she was back to work and Lilly cared for her nephew, along with all of her other miniature clients.

Lilly and Oliver's world had come crashing down around them thirteen months ago. Annie and her husband, Oliver's father, were both tragically killed in a car accident. Oliver was just six years old. Annie, ever the organised professional, had asked Lilly if she would become Oliver's legal guardian if anything were to ever happen to her and his father, one month after he was born. Lilly had scoffed at the time, telling her not to be so ridiculous - nothing was going to happen to them. But Annie was insistent, and to pacify her, of course she agreed that she would have Oliver and love him as her own. And then that day came, that hauntingly, dark, terrible day came. But thanks to Annie's pushy organisation, Oliver was instantly transitioned into her care, so that at least, was one less problem for her to deal with during the earliest grief-stricken weeks.

Everything reminded them both of Annie. Everywhere they went, everything they did, and all their favourite familiar places filled them with thoughts of Annie. The pain was too much, and the grief didn't ebb, for months. Oliver had inherited his parents' house and also received a generous sum when their life insurance policies paid out. And Annie had not forgotten Lilly. Lilly also received a sizeable sum of money.

But Lilly couldn't bear to live in Annie's house. The heartache was too great. So she and Oliver continued to live in her modest rented home, and she organised a company to let out Annie's house for the foreseeable future. Oliver could decide what to do about his parents' house once he was old enough to do so.

It was a bleak November night, seven months after the death of her sister, when everything had become too much. The rain hammered on the windows and the bitter wind howled outside, and it was then, in the solitude of her home, with only her thoughts for company whilst Oliver slept, that she came up with her plan.

 A fresh start for her and Oliver, before the new year arrived.

She needed something to focus on, they both did. She could not continue the contented little life she had carved out for herself in Dorset anymore. The memories, the constant reminders of her beloved sister, were too much to bear. Time away was what they both needed. And at the back of her mind, she knew that if it all turned out in disaster, she had her sister's house to move into and her generous sister's money to fall back on. Annie had been prepared for every eventuality, and between the heart-wrenching sobs and sips of her large glass of wine, she emailed several letting agents in Cornwall.

Cornwall wasn't too far away from Dorset. They didn't need to lose all ties with home, but it was far enough away to be a completely new start. And who didn't love Cornwall, she told herself. Picturesque beaches, exciting coastal paths for her and Oliver to explore, and the beautiful barren moors. Many adventures would be ahead of them. And distracting adventures were definitely what they both needed right now.

When she woke the next morning, she had felt a strange calmness enveloping her, and it was that feeling that encouraged her to proceed with her late-night plan, even if it was somewhat out of the box. Her sixth sense was telling her that she was doing the right thing, as scary as it was, to uproot herself and Oliver. She felt a spiritual driving force behind her, as if Annie was in agreement with her plan.

A month later, two weeks before Christmas, Lilly and Oliver moved into Pear Tree Cottage. It was a charming stone-built cottage, with a homely open fireplace, and large pear tree taking centre stage in the ample sized garden. Their new home was situated in a little Cornish village, nestled on the outskirts of the moors. Just a short five-minute walk from their little cottage, and they were on the far stretching moors and could watch the wild ponies grazing. It truly was an idyllic place to start their new lives together.

And once all the chaos of the move had passed, and they'd managed to get through Christmas, she and Oliver began to feel more settled. She had been unsure of how he would react to starting his new school mid-year. She worried that the children would have already formed their little friendship groups and Oliver would be left on his own, but she need not have been concerned about it. The quiet, little village school was exactly what Oliver needed. The local children were intrigued and friendly towards the new arrival and he was welcomed enthusiastically. The happy, inquisitive boy he had once been was beginning to emerge again. As the weeks ticked by, the pale, introverted boy he had become after the loss of his parents was slowly fading away. Lilly also knew that Isla was partly responsible for that, and she was so very grateful that she came into their lives, right when she was needed.

During one particularly brutal storm, Lilly had bundled herself into her waterproof over-clothes to brace the torrential rain and dart across their garden and into the log shed to stock up the cosy fire she had lit earlier that day. Launching herself into the shed to avoid the bombardment of heavy wind and rain, she shook herself off and took a moment to catch her breath.

And that is when she heard it. A quiet, faint cry. She froze, straining her ears to listen more clearly. There it was again. She turned towards the log pile, and there, hiding between the logs, she saw two, quizzical yellow eyes looking up at her. Speaking softly, she carefully made her way over to investigate. The drenched little cat stayed put, and let Lilly stretch out her fingers and gently stroke her. In moments the little cat was purring, grateful to receive some attention and tender affection. Lilly scooped her up, tucking her protectively under her waterproof coat, and raced back into the house. Isla and Oliver had been best friends ever since. The little cat smothered him with attention and curled up with him at bedtime, never leaving his side, all night long.

Lilly had been adamant, as soon as she brought Isla into their home that stormy night, that she was not theirs. She might have just been taking shelter from the storm, she might be someone's beloved lost pet. Oliver had nodded solemnly at her, all the while fussing over the affectionate cat. Lilly felt her sixth sense speaking to her again, that this little creature was meant to be theirs. She didn't know why or how; she just knew it. But she didn't tell Oliver that.

The next day, she contacted Rosewin Rescue, the animal shelter, situated ten minutes outside of the village. She and Oliver took her in to be checked over and to find out if she was a missing cat. Isla was found to be fit and healthy, and no one could fathom where she came from. She wasn't recognised as a local cat, no one had reported her missing, and she didn't have a microchip. Yet she appeared to be far too friendly to be a stray. She was a mystery. Lilly filled out all of the relevant paperwork and was told if no one claimed her in two weeks then Oliver could keep her.

And no one did.

Lilly knew, somehow, that this mysterious cat, arrived in her log shed for Oliver.

Oliver named her Isla after his mum. It would have been too painful to say 'Annie' out loud, but Oliver thought that her middle name, Isla, suited his new cat well. Lilly agreed. She was sure that it was Annie who had somehow brought Isla to her son.

And then something else out of the blue happened. Over the many visits to the rescue centre in a short space of time to make arrangements for Isla, she built up a rapport with one of the receptionists, and like most newcomers, the local receptionist was keen to learn all about her. And that was when she mentioned about the job. It hadn't even been advertised yet, but a member of staff's husband had just been offered a promotion, which meant that the family would have to relocate. She would be leaving in two weeks. They were desperate to fill her position - they were permanently short staffed as it was, with so many animals needing help and never enough money in the budget for extra staff.

"Rascal, put that down, you can't take that back with you!" She laughed at the little dog who was trying to drag along a stick the length of his own body. As she smiled at his antics, she still couldn't believe her luck, landing a job so easily, and a job which she thoroughly enjoyed.

Phoebe

Phoebe and Penelope trotted purposefully along the country lanes.

"Here we are girl," Phoebe announced, as they arrived at the entrance of the track that would lead them onto the moors. Turning Penelope onto the track, she encouraged a forward-going trot, and then with a gentle squeeze of her legs, they were off. Penelope's powerful legs thundered beneath her as they cantered fast along the long, winding track.

"Easy now Pen," Phoebe gently said to her horse, giving her a light squeeze of the reins to signal it was time to slow down. Breathing deeply, after their exhilarating blast, she leaned down to stroke her mare's neck, before dismounting. She fiddled with the stiff clasp of the gate before it finally wiggled free, and she could lead Penelope through the narrow, overgrown gateway, and onto the moors. Remounting, she and Penelope slowly plodded along, following the hedgerow until they found the next gateway. She brought Penelope to a halt, took a deep breath of the fresh countryside air, and enjoyed the beautiful moorland view before her. And then the silence was broken.

"Hello, are you guys there?" came a voice from behind the hedge.

"Ellen! Hi! We're ready and waiting for you two," replied Phoebe.

And then she saw Jupiter's elegant black head peer around the gateway, followed by Ellen's beaming smile.

Phoebe had met Ellen a few years ago through Joel. She'd had a rare day off and after hearing so many lovely stories about the Hollybrook ladies, she'd invited herself to tag along to work with Joel. She had been warmly welcomed by Clare, and plied with cups of tea and slices of cake. There had been lots of friendly chatting between her and all the livery ladies. *Yes,* she had thought to herself, *I can see why Joel speaks so highly of this place, and why he always enjoys his work here.*

And then Ellen had come bulldozing in, like a whirlwind, running late after a particularly busy day training a client's new horse, apologising profusely to Joel, before disappearing to catch Jupiter. Once Jupiter was safely tied up on the yard, and Joel got to work, Ellen flopped down on the haybale beside Phoebe and helped herself to the cake tin Clare had left.

"Oh yummy, chocolate brownies, my favourite!" Ellen announced, then turned to Phoebe. "Oh, hi! I'm Ellen."

"I'm Phoebe, Joel's sister." Phoebe had replied.

And that was it. They hit it off straight away and chatted nonstop until Joel had finished shoeing Jupiter. Then they had swapped numbers to organise a ride together, and they had been riding together once a week ever since.

"So, how's the new job going?" Ellen asked, bringing Jupiter alongside Penelope, so they could plod along side by side.

"My new boss is really nice, and I'm starting to find my feet now so I'm feeling a bit more settled. Miss Stillettos is still a bitch! But I avoid her as much as I can!"

"And Jack?" Ellen asked, with an arched brow.

"I knew you'd ask about him!" Phoebe laughed in reply. "He's always friendly when we see each other, but to be honest I've hardly seen him as we've been really busy landing a new client. But I'll be seeing him next weekend."

"What? Are you going on a date?" Ellen squealed in excitement.

"Oh no, wait for it," said Phoebe, pausing a beat for dramatic effect. "Team building. Bloody team building."

She waited for Ellen to finish laughing before continuing. "We were all pulled into Mr Parker's office yesterday afternoon. We got the new contract, so work is going to get crazy busy. He thought it would be a good idea for us all to have a team building weekend before the hectic workload starts. For the love of God, could you think of anything worse!" Phoebe giggled. "Going away with a load of people I don't know and having to do outdoor 'sporty' things with them!" Phoebe cringed at the thought. Horse riding was the only sport she had ever been good at, and even to use the word 'good' was generous. She lacked balance and co-ordination, as well as motivation, in truth, for any sport that didn't involve a horse.

"Two days and one night away. All we've been told is that it will be a mix of seminars and outdoor team building activities. The food had better be good," Phoebe laughed, "because quite frankly, that's the only thing I have to look forward too!"

Ellen laughed along with her. "Oh Phoebes, I'm sure it won't be all that bad, I can't wait to hear all about it!"

Pushing their horses into trot, Phoebe turned to Ellen. "Race you to the woods!" And in a split second, Penelope transitioned into a swift canter, before opening up into a fast gallop. Phoebe could hear her friend laughing and Jupiter's thundering hooves close behind.

Bridget

Bridget always looked forward to her monthly trip to Truro. She enjoyed strolling along the cobbled streets window shopping with Sally, her dearest and oldest friend. They had been friends since forever, and when they both got married and became mothers, they decided that they must always make time for themselves, and so the monthly Truro treat day was born. When their children were small, they would take them to the local park to play and eat ice creams, but now they were grown, the two of them strolled and gossiped, and then found a cosy café for lunch and more gossip.

After hugging Sally goodbye, bubbling with happiness after spending an enjoyable day with her friend, Bridget made her way to the car park. It was time to head home to William. And then she saw it, Parker Affordable Homes.

That's where Phoebe works, she thought to herself. *I wonder, would she mind if I popped in to say hello? Are mothers not allowed to do that? Would that embarrass her? But then what if she found out I was literally outside her work and didn't stop and say hello?*

Standing awkwardly outside the entrance to Parker Affordable Homes, she was saved the dilemma of making the wrong decision when a voice rang out. "Mum! What are you doing here?"

And there was Phoebe, walking straight towards her carrying two full trays of takeaway coffee, one balanced on top of the other.

"Great timing. Can you grab the door for me please?" Phoebe asked her.

Phew, Bridget thought, *she seems pleased to see me!*

"Of course, sweetheart," she replied, holding the door wide open for her. "I've just had my monthly meet-up with Sally. Would you like me to carry one of those trays?"

She saw Phoebe's eyes light up. "Would you? You don't mind? Thanks Mum," she gushed, before handing one over to her. "Come on, this way."

Bridget quietly followed, not believing her luck that Phoebe had actually invited her to step inside this world of hers that she wasn't a part of.

"Mr Parker has a meeting in five minutes. He always likes the coffee from the little shop around the corner for his important meeting. Come on Mum! Keep up!"

Bridget followed Phoebe up the stairs and through the very busy office floor. Everyone appeared to be occupied and no one seemed to notice her scuttling along behind Phoebe.

"Phoebe, there you are. Just in time," boomed Mr Parker.

Phoebe carefully placed down her tray of coffees. "Just here, Mum, next to mine," she said, gesturing with her hand where to place the tray.

"Mr Parker, this is my Mum, Bridget. Mum, this is my boss, Mr Parker," said Phoebe.

Bridget looked up at the tall, mature, handsome man standing next to her daughter. With a jolt she realised that she hadn't felt such instant attraction to anyone since her beloved Jacob. It was a strange, but not an entirely unwelcome feeling.

"Hello Bridget," Mr Parker said, holding his hand out in greeting.

"Mr Parker," she replied, as she clasped his cool, dry hand in her own.

He held her hand for just a fraction too long for a standard, formal greeting. She looked into his eyes and felt the jolt again, and she wondered if he felt it too.

"Mr Parker, it's time to start," called a voice from the nearby conference room.

The spell was broken once he released his grip from hers.

"A pleasure to meet you," he said, and then finally, dropping her gaze, he turned to Phoebe. "Come along now, Phoebe."

"I have to go now, Mum. See you at home later," she said, before dropping a quick kiss goodbye on her cheek, and she was gone.

Slightly flustered, she made her way out of the office and back onto the street. Heading back towards her car, she thought, *this has been a very strange day indeed! I must get home and tell William!*

Joel

Joel felt anticipation fizzing inside him as he pulled up outside of Rosewin rescue centre. It had been seven long days since his conversation with Rose at Hollybrook and finally, the day of his appointment with a lady called Lilly had arrived and he was about to meet Katie. He mentally prepared himself as he climbed out of his car. *She has to be the right one, and if Katie isn't it, I must be prepared for that and be patient a little while longer.* He knew that he should prepare himself for disappointment in case she wasn't the one for him, but deep down, he trusted Rose's instincts, and he was hopeful that little Katie would be the dog for him.

He pushed open the rescue centre's front door and was immediately greeted by a pretty lady behind the counter who introduced herself as Lilly.

"You must be Joel," she said, smiling at him, "I'm Lilly, we spoke on the phone a few days ago, you're right on time."

Joel nodded to return her warm welcome. He found himself quite taken back with the slim, conker brown eyed lady, with wavy golden hair worn loose around her shoulders.

"She had her final behavioural test this morning and passed with flying colours," Lilly told him proudly. "Rose said she'd explained to you that her final vet check isn't until next week."

"Yes," replied Joel, still struggling to compose himself. The anticipation of finally meeting Katie, coupled with unexpectedly meeting this attractive, friendly woman, had left him lost for words.

"Come on then, follow me, I'll take you to meet her," said Lilly.

Joel quietly followed Lilly through the door at the back of Rosewin's reception, and into a long, noisy corridor, lined with kennels filled to the brim of barking, excited dogs. Tails were wagging madly in greeting to everyone and anyone who walked past their kennels.

"Here she is," announced Lilly, sliding open Katie's kennel and gesturing for him to follow her in. "Hello, Katie," she said, bending down to stroke the little dog, "This is Joel."

On seeing Joel, Katie launched herself at him. Her little stumpy tail wagging furiously as she licked and snuffled him. "I think she likes you," laughed Lilly. "That was quite a welcome!"

Joel sat down on the cold kennel floor and let Katie climb onto his lap. After more exuberant tail wagging and snuffling, Katie circled his lap three times before promptly settling down for a nap, nestled between Joel's knees.

"What do you think of her?" Lilly tentatively asked him. He could see the hopeful, expectant look on her face. The look that told him that if this little dog found a new loving home, it would free up the kennel for another dog in need.

Joel looked at Lilly and grinned. "Oh I think Katie and I are going to get along just fine." And he was rewarded with a beaming smile from Lilly. A smile that made him feel like it wasn't just Katie that he wanted to get to know better.

"Shall we take her for a walk?" Lilly suggested. "It's always good for potential owners to get a feel of how the dog behaves out and about in the world."

At the word 'walk' Katie jumped up and started wagging her stumpy tail again. "Yes," replied Joel. "Let's take her out into the world."

Lilly clipped a lead onto Katie's collar, then handed it over to Joel. "Come along Katie, let's take Joel to your favourite place down by the river."

Katie skipped along next to Joel on her lead as Lilly led the way towards the grassy meadow, which opened up to a quiet area of riverbank where the dogs could be let off the lead in safety to play and splash in the gentle flowing water. Lilly and Joel laughed together as they watched Katie enjoying herself, zooming along the meadow bank and splashing through the water.

Joel felt Lilly's eyes move from Katie and on to himself, he turned to see her looking directly at him.

Meeting his eyes, she said, "Should I get the paperwork organised for you? You want her, don't you?"

"Very much so. She's perfect."

Smiling up at him, she said, "Let's go back then, I need some of your details to get everything started!"

Jack

"I'll be gone from Saturday morning until Sunday evening," he explained to Chloe. "I can assure you, I would much rather be here with you, letting you paint my toenails bright pink, rather than going away for this team building malarky, but Mr Parker insisted, so I'm afraid I've got to go."

Chole looked up from her magazine and giggled at him. "I could paint your nails now if you like!"

Jack burst out laughing before replying, "thanks for the offer but I think I'll decline! So, you're sure you're going to be ok?"

"For the last time Dad, yes, I'll be fine. Mum said she'd come and stay in the spare room. And if she doesn't, Meg said I can crash at hers for the weekend. All sorted."

Jack silently rolled his eyes at the thought of her mother actually committing to a plan, but Chloe was hopeful, so he didn't want to dampen her spirits. And he liked Meg, he'd met her mum a few times at the school gates and she seemed nice, so he hoped that the weekend would be spent at Meg's house, where Chloe would actually be looked after and given a decent meal.

Chloe's mother, Hazel, wasn't exactly what he would call mother material. Beautiful - hell yes. Gregarious, exciting and free spirited - most definitely. A natural mother - absolutely not. They had dated for a few months when he was twenty. A hurricane of a romance filled with passion, drama and excitement. Jack had fallen well and truly under her spell. But then Hazel fell pregnant with Chloe.

And she had tried, she really did try at being a mother, but her wandering free spirit just wouldn't allow her to settle down. When Chloe was six months old, she had handed her over to Jack and said she'd be back soon. She needed a break. A break from him and a break from their daughter. It was twelve months later when she breezed back into their lives, excitement, chaos and drama erupting in her wake. Then off again two months later. And this had been the cycle ever since. Casually flitting in and out of Chloe's life for the past sixteen years. Chloe adored her. She lived an unusual, exciting life, and would bring Chloe exotic presents and regale her with stories from her gallivants from all over the world, only ever living from one day to the next.

It was Jack who had raised her, Jack who had stayed up all night to care for her when she was unwell, who helped her with her homework, who made her packed lunches and who had been the stable, constant in her life.

And over the years, she'd said to him many times, "I love Mum, but I never want to leave you, Dad." And that was all the reward he needed.

He handed her his phone. "Just in case, can you add Meg's mums' number into my phone please. Mum might not stay the whole weekend."

Taking his phone, she punched in the number, before handing it back to him. "You're probably right, forty-eight hours might be pushing it for Mum!"

Jack slipped his phone back into his pocket and turned to head into the kitchen to get dinner started, when Chloe piped up, "How's fairy girl?"

He stopped in his tracks and replied, "Stop calling her that!" He was seriously regretting leaving his sketch book on the kitchen counter last week. He had never had any reason to hide it and Chloe often glanced through it while they chatted or pottered together in the kitchen. She was always appreciative and keen to see his drawings.

Unfortunately, his artistic talent had not been passed on to her and even stick men were a struggle for her! He often indulged her and sketched whatever she wanted him to draw. She had a folder in her room of all the silly little sketches that he had drawn for her over the years and he was secretly touched that she still kept them. Last week, she had been flicking through his sketch pad to see any new drawings and stumbled across his latest whim, the dragon and the fairy. Intrigued by the new addition, she had curiously asked the inspiration behind it. Thinking nothing of it he explained all about the new girl, the coffee-stained shirt and the cupcakes. He had foolishly forgotten the over dramatized and imaginative lives teenage girls live and thus 'fairy girl' had become of serious interest to Chloe.

"Are you going to ask her out on a date?" Chloe enquired.

"What!" he stuttered. "I barely know her!"

"Well, if you did, it would be fine by me. You hear all these terrible things that kids do when their parents start dating," she said, in a matter of fact way. "I just wanted you know that if you did want to go on a date, with fairy girl, or anyone for that matter, I'd be fine with it. I could help you pick out a shirt if you like?" she said, looking up at him, her eyes dancing as she teased him.

He looked down at his beautiful daughter. *When did she get so wise? And when the hell did we decide that we now talk about my dating life?*

"Thanks Chloe, good to know. But nothing is going on with anyone! If anything changes, you'll be the first to know, ok?"

"Ok Dad," she said, before turning her attention back to her magazine. Jack made his way into the kitchen, feeling grateful that teenagers have the attention span of a goldfish, and he could ponder in peace the idea that his daughter might be right. *Is it time to think about dating again?*

Phoebe

Phoebe pushed back the duvet and groaned. How anyone could ever, ever find this fun was beyond her. She ached all over. Even after a hot bath the night before, she had woken stff and sore.

Raft building. *I mean really, who actually cares if you can lash some barrels together and float down a river? And that water was bloody freezing!* Phoebe eased her aching limbs out of bed. *And team building, that's a laugh,* she scoffed, thinking back to when she was paired with Laura, and Laura deliberately shoved her, so she fell flat on her face in the mud when they were supposed to be working as a team to build a secure way to cross the muddy riverbank.

And she didn't like to admit it, but she was slightly disappointed not to have been paired with Jack for any of yesterday's activities. She was hoping that this time away from the office would give her a chance to get to know him a bit better. She had not forgotten his kindness to her on her fist day. She got dressed slowly, trying to put off the inevitable for as long as possible. After breakfast they were all to meet in the front lobby to be told what the torture of the day would be. *Only eight more hours to go,* she told herself, as she headed down the stairs for breakfast.

Phoebe was feeling marginally better after the delicious all you can eat buffet breakfast. Fresh fruit, scrambled eggs on toast followed by a chocolate pastry and a cup of tea had definitely perked her up. That was until the organiser attached a red band to her wrist and told her to hurry along to the lobby, as the day's activities were about to begin. Trying to quell the feeling of doom that whatever was to come would spoil her morning, she took a deep breath, and joined the rest of her colleagues.

"Good morning, all!" called out the overly enthusiastic organiser. "You were all given wristbands at breakfast. Those with a yellow band, please stand to the left

– you're all coming with me. And those with the red, wait here. Your leader will be with you shortly."

After the yellows had all been marched out of the door, Phoebe looked around her to see who awaited the same fate as her. Laura and her equally snooty sidekick, Sasha, were huddled together, deep in conversation. And then there was Jack. Her heart skipped a little beat that whatever they would be doing, she would be doing it with him. She would finally be able to spend some time with him. She smiled tentatively at him and was rewarded with one of his eye twinkling smiles in return.

"Hello, I'm Sandy, follow me to the jeep. We're off to the yard!" explained their leader for the day.

Yard? **Phoebe thought.** *Please oh please let it be a horse yard!*

During the short drive to the stables, Sandy explained all about her work with horses, and Phoebe couldn't believe her luck when she stepped onto the family run, equine therapy and horse-riding yard. They were going to spend their day with horses!

"Trust is an important part of our programme," said Sandy, the owner and therapy practitioner of the yard. "Horses are large, flight animals, and in order to form a secure partnership with them, there has to be trust on both sides. This is not a competition. All our horses have been chosen carefully for their gentle temperaments and are ideal for the job they are required to do. But they are still animals and safety is paramount at all times."

Phoebe looked around. Her colleagues were speechless and looked decidedly uneasy about spending the day with horses. Phoebe, on the other hand, could feel excitement bubbling up inside her. The sweet smell of the hay and feed coupled with the musty smell of horse sweat and leather; she breathed it all in and felt at home. She couldn't wait to get started!

Sandy led out two big, beautiful horses. A skewbald gelding who she introduced as Crackers, and a palomino mare called Isabella.

"Ok, two of you will be working with Crackers, and the other two with Issy," directed Sandy.

Phoebe hadn't taken her eyes off Isabella. She found herself being drawn to her, and she was the first to step away from the group and walk over to Issy. "I'd like to work with Isabella please?" she asked Sandy, and not once did her eyes leave the bewitching mare. She reached out her hand for the mare to sniff her in greeting, and when Issy snuffled her fingers in acceptance, Phoebe placed her hands on either side of the gentle mare's face.

She whispered to the mare, using the same quiet, soothing tone she used for Penelope, and rested her head against Issy's, they stood, quietly, just the two of them, until Sandy broke their spell by saying in a husky voice, "I think you and Issy working together is a very good idea."

They spent the morning learning how to earn trust with the horses whilst being on the ground. For Phoebe, she was just doing what she did everyday with Penelope. What she deemed as daily horse care; Leading, grooming, picking out feet and basically just being around horses. The quiet confidence she had after so many years of owning her own horse enabled her to complete each task with ease, and enjoyment. Phoebe also quickly learned that no one else in her group knew anything about horses, and after Sandy paired her with Jack, she did everything she could to help him feel at ease around them. Phoebe was so submerged in her equine world that she didn't even think about being shy and nervous around Jack. She was in her comfort zone, and her experience and passion for horses took over and she was able to be completely herself around him. And she was finding that she very much enjoyed his company. Work wise, he was her senior, but here, on the yard, he was putting his trust in her to keep him safe, and she was not going to let him down.

After a hearty lunch, enjoyed by everyone in Sandy's welcoming family kitchen, the afternoon's activity was to be riding.

"Now remember, each of us have a different mountain to climb. Just sitting on a horse might be the top of the mountain for one and cantering without a saddle might be the top for someone else. This is about our own goals, no one else's," announced Sandy.

Everyone looked solemnly at Sandy and nodded.

"Laura and Sasha, you two are up first," said Sandy, gesturing for them to follow her into the sand school with Crackers. Phoebe and Jack took their seats to watch quietly.

"You are wonderful with horses," Jack said to her. "A real natural."

Phoebe felt her face flush under his praise. *If only he knew that I am what one would call an adequate rider,* she thought. If he wanted to see a true horseman at work, Joel was the one to watch.

"My brother, Joel, taught me how to ride. He's the real horseman. He lives and breathes horses, and works with them too. They are his life. For me, they are a passion, but I'm afraid I still have a lot to learn," she humbly explained to him.

"Do you have your own horse?" Jack enquired.

Bursting with pride, Phoebe announced, "Her name is Penelope. Joel trained her for me – well, he trained us both!"

They both looked up to see Laura, beaming like a Cheshire cat, sitting on top of Crackers, being led around the arena by Sandy.

"Oh look at her," squeaked Phoebe, smiling and waving to Laura. "Isn't she doing brilliantly!"

"It's our turn now, come on," Phoebe told Jack as soon as she saw Sandy wave them over.

Phoebe stood by Issy's head. "I promise you, I've got her," she said, holding firmly to the lead rope. "You can trust us, Jack."

Phoebe thought that Jack looked rather pale, but his foot was resting in the stirrup, and all he had to do was swing his leg over and he'd be sitting on Issy.

"On my count, one, two, three..." And she watched as Jack swung his leg over a horse for the first time. "You did it! How do you feel?"

Jack looked down at her and grinned. "Let's go for a walk," he replied.

Phoebe was thrilled for her colleagues after watching them all enjoy their first horse ride. And now it was her turn to ride in front of everyone. And she felt a little bit sick. She battled constantly with her own confidence and inadequacies, but she always had Joel to jolly her along. Except, he wasn't here today. With everyone's eyes on her, she climbed up onto the mounting block and slid her leg over Issy. Phoebe had been instructed that she would be riding without a saddle. She could already ride, and she must build her trust with Issy and push her own boundaries.

As soon as she felt the strength and warmth of Issy's back beneath her, she relaxed. She had ridden Penelope many times without a saddle, but only ever Penelope. She had never trusted another horse like she did Pen, but Issy's steady walk built her confidence until she was ready to give her the cue to transition up to trot. Her transition was smooth, and it only took Phoebe a split second to adjust to her movement and regain her balance. Focused only on Issy, Phoebe trotted in circles and figures of eight around the sand school, the steady mare keeping a comfortable pace. And then she felt it, the trust between her and this spellbinding mare, and she asked her to canter. Effortlessly, Issy transitioned into an elegant rocking horse canter and Phoebe felt like they were dancing a dance that only the two of them knew the steps too. Aside from Pen, she had never felt a connection like it with another horse, and she was truly grateful that Issy had shown her that she could trust another horse just like her beloved Penelope, if she wanted to.

Lilly

Lilly felt an excitement that she hadn't felt in a long time when she and Oliver sat down at their little kitchen table for breakfast. She was eagerly waiting for news from Rose about a new rescue dog that she had fallen in love with, and today, Joel would be coming to collect Katie. As much as she didn't like to admit it to herself, she was secretly looking forward to seeing him again. And although she knew she'd live to regret it when she came home covered in slobber and pet hair, she couldn't help herself and had deliberately chosen to wear her second favourite lilac shirt to work that day. *My absolute favourite would just be silly, I'm not prepared to get that covered in dog slobber for any man!* she chuckled to herself.

After safely dropping Oliver at school, Lilly headed to work with a spring in her step. She completed her normal routine of checking her emails and double checking the diary appointments for the day, and then she was finally able to go and see Milo. She opened his kennel door and enveloped him in a huge hug and smothered him in kisses. She whispered in his ear, "I hope you will be mine; I hope you will be coming home with me very soon."

Milo was a friendly, well-behaved golden Labrador. He had come into Rosewin five days ago after his elderly owner had tragically passed away. With no immediate family available to take on Milo, he had been handed over to Rosewin. Lilly's heart had gone out to him. She knew how devastating it was to lose a loved one, and Milo was withdrawn and missing his owner terribly. Ever since he had arrived at Rosewin, Lilly had felt a connection with him, and she had tentatively made enquiries to Andrew and Rose if she and Oliver might be considered as his potential new owners. His easy going, friendly temperament meant that he could come to work with her every day. He could snooze under her desk and accompany her on her many daily walks. The only question was, would he get along with Isla? She couldn't possibly bring a dog into her home that might frighten her or chase her.

Andrew and Rose had been thrilled at the possible idea and agreed that he must be tested with cats before any decision was made. And of course, they needed to follow the rescue centre procedure of general behavioural assessments and veterinary checks before they could sign him ff.

She clipped on his lead, and said "Come along Milo, it's time for your walk." And with Milo happily trotting along beside her, Lilly's mind began to wander to Joel.

Joel was scheduled to collect Katie at the end of the day. He'd explained that an evening collection would be best. He wanted to take her straight home to get settled before her life began as his companion and van dog. She would be accompanying him on his very busy, and often hectic days travelling from yard to yard as a farrier. Lilly was too ashamed to admit that she had absolutely no idea what a farrier was, and so she had googled it as soon as she had got home from work after the first time she had met Joel.

He shoes horses! She finally understood. And now it all made sense, everything Rose had said about him spending a lot of time on the yard. *These horsey lot speak a different language to the rest of us!* she had thought to herself after finally putting all the pieces of the puzzle together.

"It also explains the somewhat rugged, yet masculine appearance he has," she confided to Milo. She pictured him in her mind, his messy, auburn coloured hair sticking up in all directions. Well-worn jeans matched with a flannel checked shirt covered his tall broad frame, and he had tanned, weathered skin from a lifetime of working outside. She also liked the quiet, calm way he had with Katie.

I guess to be a farrier he must be good with animals, she thought happily, *and Katie will be going to a wonderful home, and that is what it is all about.*

Andrew was waiting for her when she returned. He told her that Rose had pulled some strings and managed to get Tara, Rosewin's canine behaviouralist, to assess Milo the previous evening.

"And after Tara signed him off as being safe to be rehomed with a cat, Rose couldn't help herself!" Andrew told her with a smile. "She was here at seven o'clock this morning to give Milo his vet assessment, and he passed with flying colours! She said to tell you that he's all yours! I've just finished writing up his paperwork. Once you've signed it, Milo can go home with you."

"Oh, how wonderful!" squealed Lilly. "I can't wait to tell Oliver! I didn't want to say anything until it was all one hundred percent agreed!"

Lilly spent the rest of her day in a bubble of happiness. After all the dogs had been given their walk, and Sooty, the tiny, non-descript breed dog who looked like an adorable little black puff ball on legs, was collected by his new forever family, Lilly was finally able to retrieve Milo.

My own dog! she thought gleefully as she settled him under her desk in his brand-new bed.

"No more kennels for you," she explained to him. "You are part of the Rosewin Rescue team now! I'm going to pronounce you head of the welcoming committee; your job is to wag your tail and be friendly to anyone and everyone who comes in, ok?" Milo looked up at her, then licked her nose. "I'll take that as a yes then!"

Milo and Lilly heard the front door open, and whilst Lilly attempted to straighten herself out from sitting under her desk with her dog, Milo leapt into action and bounded towards his first visitor as head of Rosewin's welcoming committee.

Lilly felt her heart skip a beat at the sound of Joel's voice. "Hello boy, who are you? Should you be out here all on your own?" she heard him say to Milo

"He's mine," Lilly called out, still on her hands and knees. Hastily running her fingers through her hair and praying that she didn't look like a complete train wreck, she finally stood up and revealed herself from behind the reception desk. She saw Joel crouching down, scratching Milo behind his ears as the dog stared adoringly at him. *If only we could all be like dogs and so open with our affections* she thought wryly.

"Hi Joel," Lilly said, and then felt her cheeks flush when he turned his attention to her and greeted her with his gentle smile. "His name is Milo," she stammered, trying to push her way through the hurricane of feelings she felt whizzing through her that she most definitely did not have time to process now. "He's one of ours but I officially become his owner today."

"Congratulations, so we will both be taking dogs home with us today!" Joel replied, grinning broadly as he made his way over to her. "And how is Katie? Is she ready?"

"She's ready and waiting! Let's go and get her." Lilly led Joel to Katie's kennel, opened the door, then stood back and watched Katie hurtle herself at Joel. She launched herself into his arms, her little body wriggling with excitement under all the attention he lavished on her.

"I think she's happy to see you," Lilly remarked. Joel gave her a bashful smile as the little dog continued her exuberant idolisation of Joel.

"You just need to sign her paperwork, then she's all yours!" Lilly said.

Katie and Milo introduced themselves and then set about exploring the reception area together whilst Lilly organised the paperwork. Joel was standing right next to her, and she felt her pulse quicken at being in such close proximity to him. And when his hand grazed hers as he took the pen from her, she felt like she had been hit by an electric bolt. *What is it about this man? I can barely think straight when I'm around him! Now pull yourself together,* she chastised herself, *and start behaving in a professional manner.*

"All done," Lilly announced, "Katie is officially yours."

Joel scooped up his little dog, "Thank you for everything, Lilly. I'd better get her home, she has a busy day ahead of her tomorrow." And with a final, knee-weakening smile, which Lilly felt Joel held just that little bit too long for it to be one hundred percent professional, Joel and Katie left.

"Oh Milo," Lilly said, wrapping her arms around him and burying her head in his soft, silky fur, "this is not good, I'm a full-grown woman with a crush! Could my life get any more embarrassing!" Milo licked her cheek and thumped his tail. "We'd better go home; Oliver is going to be so thrilled to meet you!"

Jack

It was Saturday night and with Chloe out at the cinema with one of her girlfriends, Jack was alone with a glass of whiskey, his sketch pad laid open in front of him, and a pencil idle in his hand. It had been one week since the work team building weekend, and Jack could not get the picture of Phoebe and Isabella out of his mind.

The past week at work had been full on. The new contract took precedence over everything, which had kept him focused and busy. But if he looked up from his desk and saw her, or bumped into her around the office, his mind became flooded with the images of her and the golden horse and the mystical partnership they created. He couldn't stop thinking about the beauty of them riding together; Jack had never seen anything like it.

Mr Parker was keeping them all on a tight schedule, so he hadn't had a chance to speak to her other than the briefest greeting. Only once had he been able to slip out of the office to buy a decent cup of coffee and he returned with one for Phoebe, an excuse to speak to her, but he had been cut short. As soon as he had handed the coffee over to her and been rewarded with her genuine appreciation and friendly smile, Mr Parker had whisked her away from him.

He was unused to the feelings that Phoebe seemed to have unleashed within him. It had been just him and Chloe for so long, and the strong pull of attraction he felt for Phoebe was unexpected. He was finding himself in unchartered territory.

He slowly weaved his pencil between his fingers and sipped his whiskey. *It's time,* he thought to himself. He felt the pencil jump into life as soon as the lead touched the paper. The images he had memorised came spilling out of him. With each stroke of the pencil, each carefully crafted angle, each softly sketched curve and his blushed blending and shades, the girl and the horse appeared before him. There she was, her head resting against Issy's, her hands on either side of the gentle mare's face, and they were at peace. A peace that Jack sensed he had never felt before. A sense of trust and security that only Phoebe and Issy could feel. And a feeling of unequivocal contentment between them. And Jack wondered, *what might it feel like for Phoebe to place her soft hands on him, just like she had on the horse?*

He thought back to how she had blossomed in the company of the horses. It was like she was being her true self. The Phoebe that was kept at bay in work hours because of the snide, bossy, over-opinionated Laura and Sasha. And then Jack smiled to himself as he remembered how kind and supportive Phoebe had been when the snarky duo slowly gained confidence around the horses and then eventually rode them. *A testament to her genuine character,* Jack thought. *Those women have been nothing but awful to her since meeting her, but she still encouraged and supported them.*

His pencil sprang back into life again as he placed it on a new, blank sheet of paper. His creativity was not yet sated. His mind steadied and focused, like it always did when he drew, and the feminine curves of both Phoebe and Issy appeared on to the paper. In his mind's eye he could see them cantering around the sand school. He could feel the warmth spread within him as he remembered watching such elegance, and his pencil enabled him to bring his memories to life.

Lost in his own world, he was startled when he heard the front door slam and Chloe's bubbling voice echoed through from the hallway, calling him.

"Dad, I'm home. I've brought you my left-over pic n mix! Oh, there you are," she said, planting a kiss on top of his head and dropping the sweets next to him.

Jack hastily tried to hide his drawings away. He was unsure of his own feelings, and he did not want to confuse Chloe, and he told himself that in reality, there wasn't anything going on anyway! Nothing to talk about, least of all to his daughter.

"Oh, you've been drawing. Can I see?" enquired Chloe.

"How was the movie?" he asked, trying to change the subject.

"Great, we both really enjoyed it, happy ending romantic comedy. You'd have loathed it!" she laughed in reply. "So can I see?" she asked, gesturing towards his sketch book.

Jack swiftly weighed up his options. Denying her a peek at his sketches would just intensify her curiosity and imply that something was going on. *Which it most definitely isn't,* he reminded himself. Or he could show her an innocent drawing of a woman and a horse from his weekend away because he had nothing better to do with his time due to being ditched by his beloved daughter on a Saturday night. He went with the latter and handed over his sketch pad.

"Oh, Dad," Chloe gasped, "these are brilliant." And she lifted them up towards the light and drank in every detail of his tender, heartfelt, talented drawings. "Truly wonderful."

Jack became self-conscious under his daughter's praise of his very private drawings. Taking a generous swig from his whiskey, he offered, "It's the horse from the work weekend."

"Work weekend," Chloe murmured, still staring at the picture. "This is one of the women you work with?"

And before he had chance to answer, he saw her mentally piecing it all together, "Oh my, this is fairy girl!"

Blushing for the second time in front of his daughter, he distracted himself by taking the final swig of whiskey from his glass before strolling over to his drinks cabinet for a refill.

"She's really pretty, Dad, and she rides horses! She seems really cool," enthused Chloe. "Do you like her?"

"She's a work colleague," was all he deemed necessary as a reply.

Chole looked up at him. "It's ok if you like her dad," she said softly.

Jack was lost for words, and without breaking eye contact with his daughter, took another swig of whiskey. *Bloody hell,* he thought, *I'll be pissed before I've managed to get through this if I don't bring this conversation to an end very quickly!*

Ignoring Jack's discomfort, Chloe ploughed on. "If you like fairy girl, or if you met someone in general, and you went on a date, I'd been fine with it. I want you to be happy." And then she reached up on her tip toes and planted a kiss on his cheek before turning on her heel and casually sauntering out of the sitting room.

Just as Jack was trying to comprehend what his daughter had so eloquently expressed to him, her head popped around the sitting room door.

"And if you want my opinion," said Chloe.

"Which I haven't asked for!" he quipped.

His joking tone encouraged Chloe to roll her eyes at him before stating, "If you like her, you should give her the picture." And with the air of a know-it-all teenage girl, she finished with, "Girls like that sort of thing, it's romantic."

After he heard her clomping up the stairs, and the sound of her favourite music softly flowing out of her bedroom, Jack finally closed his eyes to mull over Chloe's suggestion. *Should he give Phoebe the drawing?*

Bridget

Sitting at her kitchen table, sipping her morning cup of tea, Bridget was feeling somewhat disappointed. Today was her monthly lunch date with Sally, but she had just received a message from her offering her apologies, but she would not be able to meet her today. Her daughter, accompanied by suitcases and her cat, had just arrived on her doorstep. She was both devastated and distraught as she had just discovered that her long-term boyfriend, and the love of her life, had been cheating on her for the past six months. Sally promised to keep Bridget updated and said she would message again soon.

Bridget was heartbroken for Sally's daughter and totally understood why the lunch date had been cancelled. She would have done exactly the same if it had been Phoebe or Joel. But it did leave her feeling deflated. She always enjoyed her time with Sally and knowing that she was due to see her friend today, Joel had kindly fed and groomed William, then turned him out in the paddock with Eliza and Penelope for her, so she didn't even have her daily yard chores to occupy her.

After a leisurely breakfast she finally came up with a plan. She would go to Truro anyway. She would stroll along the high street to do some window shopping and then she would idle away some time choosing a new book for herself from her favourite book shop. Then she would enjoy a cup of tea and a slice of cake from a cosy café before heading home. *Yes,* she thought, *a day in Truro can still be enjoyable on my own.*

Bridget clutched her glossy carrier bag containing two new books. *Two books!* she thought, *I really have spoiled myself today!* And she pushed open the door to a little café tucked away from the main street. The smell of fresh coffee and home baked treats wafted towards her as soon as she entered and made her way over to the counter. Her mouth watered at the sight of all the tasty cakes on display before her.

"One cup of tea and a slice of lemon cake please," she told the expectant server.

Bridget had just got herself settled at a little table next to the window, always her favourite place to sit so she could enjoy watching the world go by, when a familiar figure walked through the door.

Blimey, she thought, *that's Phoebe's boss. What on earth is he doing here?* And she tentatively pulled out her compact mirror from her handbag and subtly checked her makeup. Feeling self-conscious, she looked up to see if he had spotted her, or if indeed he recognised her at all. *You've only met him once,* she told herself. *He's a busy man, I doubt he will remember me,* she thought, trying to save herself from disappointment if he were to ignore her. But she couldn't help remembering that their first meeting had left a lasting impression on her.

Her inner self doubt was unfounded, and she was greatly relieved when Mr Parker weaved his way between the tables towards her.

"Phoebe's mum," he stated. "Bridget, isn't it?"

Feeling like a teenager being acknowledged by her crush, Bridget replied, "Yes, that's right. Hello Mr Parker."

Smiling down at her, holding his cup of coffee, he asked, "Are you alone?"

"Yes, my friend had a family emergency so I'm on my own today," she explained.

"Would you mind if I joined you?" Mr Parker ventured.

Not believing her own luck, Bridget moved her coat and carrier bags off the spare seat and gestured for Mr Parker to sit down.

Settled in the welcoming street café, Bridget and Mr Charles Parker, spent a very enjoyable hour getting to know one another. It transpired that Charles was also widowed and his wife had passed away six years ago. He had initially thrown himself into his work to help control his grief, but as time went on, he began to find little things in life that brought him joy again. In his spare time, he very much enjoyed long countryside walks or rolling his trousers up and walking bare foot across the beach feeling the cool water on his skin. He was also intrigued to hear all about William!

The sound of his phone ringing brought them both back down to reality. Mr Parker was needed back at work, but he did not leave without asking if he might be permitted her phone number, and if she would like to meet up with him again?

Excitement fizzed through her as she carefully wrote down her phone number for him and she received a warm smile from him when she handed it to him.

"Goodbye Bridget, and thank you for a lovely afternoon," said Charles, and he gave her arm an affection pat before heading back off to work.

Bridget felt the same jolt from his touch as she had the first time. *There is definitely something intriguing about that man*, she thought, *and I'm very much looking forward to seeing him again!*

Joel

Joel and Eliza were idling along a quiet track in the woods as Katie zoomed about in every direction having the time of her life. There were so many things to investigate that she didn't know which way to go first. She scurried about all over the place, forwards and backwards, zig zagging in and out of the trees, down rabbit holes and through the bushes. Joel couldn't believe how much energy she had!

Katie never went out of calling distance though. She idolised Joel and was never too far from his side, no matter how tantalising a scent was for her to follow, which made it safe for her to run loose alongside Joel and Eliza in the quiet woods. Joel watched the little dog catch a scent and whizz off into the distance. He couldn't believe how lucky he was to have her. She was the perfect companion, well behaved with clients, and if for any reason a client didn't want her loose on their yard, she snoozed quietly in his van until it was time to leave. Rose had matched them up perfectly, and he was so very grateful to her.

Relaxing to the gentle rhythm of Eliza's steady footsteps beneath him, he reflected that finding Katie had also meant that he had found Lilly. Katie had been with him for two weeks now, and still he thought of Lilly, Rosewin's enchanting receptionist. He had not forgotten how adorable she looked crawling out from Milo's bed beneath her desk with her crumpled clothes and messy hair. He didn't think he had ever seen anyone more beautiful. And what a jolt he had felt when he accidentally brushed her hand! He found himself hoping that she had felt it too. But between his busy work schedule and reserved nature, he had so far struggled to come up with an excuse to accidentally bump into her again at Rosewin.

He heard the sound of thundering little paws headed in his direction, pulling his mind from thoughts of Lilly he looked across and saw Katie hurtling towards him, with a golden Labrador hot on her heels. *A Labrador that looks suspiciously like Milo*, he thought, when he caught site of the blue and white checked collar he was wearing, identical to the one Milo sported the first time he met him. But no sign of Lilly. Dismounting from Eliza, he greeted Milo. "Where's your mistress Milo?" he asked, looking in every direction, but still unable to see Lilly.

After greeting Joel, Milo and Katie blasted off in the direction they had come from. They stopped and turned, enticing Joel to follow. He swiftly climbed back into his saddle so he and Eliza could follow the dogs. The dogs were hurtling along the woodland track forcing Eliza to pick up a steady canter to keep pace with them. Panting heavily after their long sprint, the dogs finally slowed and led Joel down a narrow track, and that is when he saw her.

"Lilly," he called out, at the same time as swinging his leg over his saddle and athletically landing on the ground. "Are you ok? What happened?"

"Joel, am I pleased to see you! I thought no one would find me down here. I tripped and fell; I must have twisted my ankle because I can't walk on it."

"Milo found me and brought me to you. You're lucky to have such a loyal dog," Joel replied, as he affectionately stroked Milo. "Here, let me help you up." And in one smooth movement he lifted her up from the awkward position on the ground and held her in his arms. With her head leaning on his chest, he could smell the light flowery fragrance of her perfume and feel the warmth of her body pressed against him. He didn't want to put her down.

"Lilly, meet Eliza, your ride home," he announced, as he carried her over to his horse. He suddenly felt her blanch at being brought into such close proximity with his horse. "She's very friendly," he hastily added. "And safe, she won't hurt you."

"I've never ridden a horse before," Lilly whispered. "I've never actually been this close to one. I've only ever petted them over a fence. And Eliza seems to be a very big one," she stated, with a quiver of fear in her voice.

Joel sometimes forgot that some people's lives didn't revolve around horses. Not only did he have Eliza, but he worked with horses too, and every single one of his clients' lives revolved around their horses. His whole life was horses, and he felt wrong-footed for presuming Lilly would be happy to ride Eliza home. And guilty for making that presumption.

"If you say I can trust her, I'll ride her," Lilly said tentatively. "I need to get home somehow, and my own two feet aren't going to get me there!" she admitted in a wry tone.

Taking one last breath of her intoxicating, feminine, flowery scent, Joel reluctantly lifted her on to Eliza, who didn't move a muscle the entire time it took for Lilly to get comfy and settled in her saddle. Holding on tightly to Eliza's mane, Lilly nodded to Joel. He took hold of the reins and gently asked Eliza to walk on. Walking alongside Eliza, with the two dogs zooming about in every direction, Joel asked, "Which way are we going?"

"Just down there," Lilly said, pointing along an open track. "My cottage is about a half an hour's walk from here."

Once they had set off in the correct direction, Lilly volunteered, "It was my own fault," she said, gesturing to her ankle. "I've had a lot on my mind, I was miles away and not concentrating on where I was going. I tripped over a large tree root, lost my footing, and slipped down that little track you found me on. I'm so grateful Milo found you and brought you to me."

Joel turned to look at her. "I'm pleased it was me who found you," he said, meeting her eyes and returning her shy smile. He felt himself blush after the brief moment they just shared. A moment where he sensed that she could see right through him. That she could feel the intensity that he felt when he was near her. To hide his burgeoning emotions, he blurted out, "The thing that's on your mind. Anything I can help you with?"

"It's work," Lilly admitted. "Budget cuts and funding cuts, it's always an ongoing cycle. So many animals needing help and not enough money for us to help them all. I've been trying to come up with ideas that could bring some much-needed money into Rosewin. If we don't find some extra money from somewhere we are going to have to turn animals away," she said gravely.

"What about a fundraising fete?" Joel suggested.

"That was my first idea," Lilly admitted, "But we would need lots of stalls, a games area, catering choices, an ice cream van, wash facilities, car parking, and all of those things take up a lot of space! I haven't been able to find anywhere large enough to cater for what we would need." Before Joel had a chance to reply, she blurted out, "Oh look, we're here. That's my house with the blue front door."

Joel carefully manoeuvred Eliza through the little garden gate and halted her right outside Lilly's front door. He felt his heart quicken as he placed his arms around her again to carefully lift her off Eliza. Holding her close to him, he carried her into her home and gently placed her down on her comfy looking sofa. Milo followed them inside and positioned himself firmly next to his mistress, and Katie, exhausted from her walk, promptly flopped down in Milo's bed beside the fireplace and fell asleep.

"You need to rest your ankle," he announced. "Shall I make you a cup of tea, can I get you anything?"

"A cup of tea would be lovely, thank you," she replied. "And make one for you too, it's the least I can offer after all you have done for me."

Finding his way around her little kitchen, he noticed children's drawings adorning the fridge, and little shoes strewn by the back door. Carrying two cups of tea into the sitting room he asked, "You have a child?"

"Yes, my nephew, Oliver." And as he settled himself on the armchair opposite her, enjoying his much-needed cup of tea, he listened to her explain about how

Oliver became hers. As her story unfolded it took all of his strength to remain seated, barely five feet away from her, when deep down he felt a compelling sensation to take her in his arms and hold her. To protect from all the hurt and heartache she had suffered.

He found himself without words after hearing the tale of her tragedy, and he felt an unexplainable driving force to try and help her in any way he could. He knew he couldn't change the past, but if he could do anything to ease her discomfort now, he would do it.

"Your fundraising fete," he said. "You could hold it my place if you'd like to?"

Phoebe

Phoebe placed her arms around Penelope, buried her face in her mane and breathed deeply. The heavenly horsey smell never failed to bring a sense of calmness and peace to her. And calmness was very much needed right now. Jack would be arriving in half an hour.

Phoebe opened up the grooming box, chose Penelope's favourite brush, and with the relaxing rhythmical strokes of the brush, she divulged the latest 'Jack gossip' to her most faithful friend, trusting her implicitly not to breathe a word to anyone.

Three days ago, just as she was leaving the office to head home, Jack had called out to her. "Phoebe, hi, I've been waiting for you. I've hardly seen you since the teambuilding weekend and I wanted to give you this," he said, handing her an envelope. "It's not work related," he hurriedly told her. "It's -" he stammered. "Well, you'll find out once you open it."

Intrigued, and secretly thrilled that Jack had stopped her for a personal matter, Phoebe replied, "Can I open it now?"

"Of course, here, sit down," Jack said, as he gestured for them both to sit on the wooden bench, situated on the quiet cobbled street, near the office.

Phoebe slowly peeled open the envelope and slid out the drawing. Her breath caught in her throat as she held the exquisite artwork in her hands. "You drew this?" she asked him. She acknowledged his nod before returning her attention back to the captivating sketch. No one had ever given her such an enchanting, thoughtful gift. She felt a swell of emotions building inside her and devoured every inch of the intricate drawing of Isabella and herself. The picture not only offered a detailed depiction of her and Issy, but it also captured the emotions she had felt, and she was sure Issy also felt, at the exact moment when they sensed the trust between them and cantered as one. She couldn't believe how talented Jack was.

"This is the most beautiful gift I have ever received," she had told him when she finally manged to tear her eyes away from the picture and look at Jack. And then she felt her emotions get the better of her as a tear silently slipped down her flushed cheek. Without saying a word, Jack reached out his hand and gently wiped away her tear with hisfinger.

"I'm pleased you like it," he said in a gruff voice, before slowly removing his hand and placing it next to hers on the bench.

She recounted the whole story to Penelope. "And then we talked and talked. He told me all about his daughter, Chloe. I told him all about you! And losing Dad. And then, Penelope, I invited Jack to come and meet you!" Phoebe heard a car pulling up to the yard, "Yikes Pen. That will be him now." Phoebe unlatched the stable door and led Penelope onto the yard.

"Hi Jack," she called out, waving to him as he climbed out of his car. "Welcome to Pine Trees."

"Wow," exclaimed Jack. "What a magnificent horse," he enthused, stepping onto the yard to greet Phoebe and Penelope. "She's big!"

"She's super friendly," Phoebe gushed, gesturing for Jack to come closer. "Hold out your hand and let her sniff you." And she watched Jack break into a smile when Penelope's whiskers gently tickled his outstretched hand. "She likes you!"

"Come on, follow us," Phoebe announced. "I'm just going to turn her out into her paddock with my mum's pony, William. You can meet him too."

Phoebe and Jack leant against the gate and watched the horses graze in silence, both quietly appreciating the unspoilt view before them. Pretty meadows, separated by smart post and rail fences, a gentle flowing stream marking their boundary, and across the river, the pine trees. Hundreds and hundreds of them, creating a mystical atmosphere of wonder and excitement of what they might contain. What adventure she and Penelope might enjoy next. She breathed in deeply and smelt the familiar sweet, fresh air.

"My paradise," Phoebe said, finally breaking the stillness of the air.

"Indeed, it is," Jack replied.

"It's a bit of a project!" Phoebe said, casting her eyes over her paradise in one direction and a building site in the other.

"Pine Trees will be amazing once it's all finished. Who's that?" Jack asked, pointing to a horse and rider emerging from the trees a little way up the stream.

"That's Joel, my brother, and his horse Eliza. I'll introduce you."

Back on the yard, Phoebe introduced the two men, who both nodded and shook hands in acknowledgement of each other, although Joel seemed to be somewhat distracted.

"Phoebes, I'm glad I caught you, I've been meaning to talk to you about something," said Joel.

Phoebe was busy explaining the different grooming brushes to Jack as she showed him how to groom Eliza down after her ride.

"I might have said to someone that we would hold a fundraiser for Rosewin rescue centre at Pine Trees," he admitted.

"Really? How exciting," said Phoebe. "It will be a brilliant way to celebrate after a year of building work, when Pine Trees is finally finished, and make some money for the animal centre too. Great idea, Joel!"

That was when she noticed Joel looking shifty and avoiding making eye contact with her. "You do mean in twelve months, don't you, when everything's finished?"

"Well, I...um...well," he stammered.

"Spit it out Joel!"

"Four weeks," he said with a guilty tinge in his voice.

"Joel," said Phoebe, and with a sweeping gesture of her arm, "Pine Trees is a building site! The only bathroom we have is in the farmhouse and quite frankly it's a bit of a death trap to get to, isn't it?"

"Yes, I'm not disagreeing with you, but the rescue centre is in trouble. They're at the point where they will have to turn animals away if they don't raise the money. I was thinking that we could have it in the top paddocks. One for parking and one for the fete, no one would be anywhere near our building site!"

Phoebe mulled over the idea, and she quietly agreed that it could be done without anyone venturing down to the yard. And the thought of animals not getting the help they needed weighed heavily on her. *But could it be organised in just four weeks?*

"Ok," she said to Joel, "I'm in. What's the plan then?"

"Well, first of all we need to get as many people as possible to help us, so rally up your friends!" Joel replied, grinning broadly at her.

"I can help," said Jack, "and I'm sure Chloe would love to be involved too."

Phoebe was touched, yet again, by the thoughtful man she was becoming friends with. Hopefully more than friends. "I'd like that," she said, smiling shyly at him, "thank you."

Lilly

Lilly surveyed her sitting room and nodded to herself in approval.

I think everything is ready, she thought, going over everything one last time. White board and markers – check. Note-pads and pencils – check. List of fundraising ideas – check. List of volunteers confirmed to man stalls, run games and be general helpers – check. Oliver, Isla and Milo all present and correct – check. Overflowing platters of cocktail pasties collected from the local bakery on her way home from work this evening – check!

She turned to her three little helpers. "Ok, team. Milo, you're on welcoming duties. Isla, you're on socialising duties and Oliver, your job is to offer everyone pasties."

Three pairs of eyes looked solemnly at her before Oliver replied, "We won't let you down Aunty Lilly."

Right on time, Lilly heard a knock. "Someone's here!" she announced, making her way to the front door. "Joel, welcome, come in on," said Lilly, holding the door wide open for him and Katie. As he brushed passed her to squeeze into her little hallway, she noticed his still damp hair and the subtle scent of fresh soap and clean clothes. She quickly noted that he did not have the usual horsey aroma about him, nor was he wearing weather beaten work clothes. Lilly felt herself blush. He looked even more handsome in his casual, clean jeans and his forest green cotton shirt.

A friendly lady bustled in behind Joel carrying Tupperware containers. "I hope you don't mind me tagging along. I'm Bridget, Joel's mum," she said, introducing herself.

Lilly was grateful for the distraction of meeting her from the overflowing emotions that seemed to flood her every time she was around Joel, and she returned Bridget's friendly smile. "The more the merrier, let me help you," she said, relieving Bridget of one of the large containers. "Cupcakes," Bridget announced. "I thought everyone might need some sustenance with all the work ahead of us this evening!"

Touched by her thoughtful gesture, Lilly replied, "How kind of you. Come on in and meet Oliver."

No sooner had she shown Bridget and Joel into her sitting room and introduced them to Oliver, Phoebe and Jack arrived. It wasn't long before all introductions had been completed. Isla made herself comfortable on Phoebe's lap, Milo and Katie curled up on the floor at Joel's feet, and they were all settled with cups of tea and tasty snacks. The Rosewin rescue fete meeting began.

Lilly's cosy little sitting room became a hive of excited chatter as they all shared their ideas, and plans began to take shape. Lilly was thrilled with Phoebe and Jack's inspiring idea of auctioning sketches of the rescue animals currently residing at Rosewin, patiently hoping that they would find their forever home soon. Flicking through some of Jack's sketches she was bowled over with how talented he was, and she knew he would do each and every animal justice, and hopefully add much needed pennies to the fundraising pot as well. A date was set up for him to visit Rosewin and meet his muses.

Joel was the designated car parking attendant, a job that was far more important than people realised. It was imperative that everyone was organised on arrival. A smooth transition from car to fete was needed to ensure happy fete-goers, because everyone knew that happy people would have much deeper pockets than grumpy, frustrated ones. Joel was to make sure all cars flowed fluidly, right up until the moment that they reached their designated parking spot.

Phoebe and her friend Ellen would be manning the pony station. Little William and little Pipsqueak, an adorable Shetland pony belonging to Hollybrook stables, generously being loaned out for the fete, would be available for children and adults alike to meet, pet and groom for a small donation.

Volunteers from Rosewin were organising the games, and a catering van, ice cream van and bouncy castle had all been hired for the special day. And on hearing the fete was to be in aid of an animal shelter, all the suppliers had generously offered their services at a greatly lowered price, thus substantially reducing their overhead costs.

Bridget would be heading up the cake stall. Her delicious cakes were legendary, and she was unanimously voted to be the best woman for the job. Lilly noticed how she had glowed under the praise Joel and Phoebe showered her with when it came to her excellent cooking and baking skills. And after sampling the selection of the sweet treats she had shared with them all that evening, Lilly had no doubt that her cakes would literally sell like hot cakes!

The final point raised on the agenda was marketing. Everything was heading in the direction of a fantastic fete, an enjoyable day out for all the family, but what good would it be if no one knew about it? Marketing was now the most important thing to focus on. The fete would be held in just three weeks. They bounced ideas and suggestions between them, each person offering to do their bit towards advertising and marketing.

Bridget caught Lilly's eye and beckoned her over. "I think this little man is ready for bed," she said in hushed tones. Oliver was curled up next to her, snuggled under her arm, fast asleep. *He looks so beautiful when he's sleeping,* Lilly thought, bending down to pick him up.

She felt a shadow fall over her as Joel's large frame silently appeared beside her. "Here, let me," he whispered, slipping his arms around the sleeping boy, and carefully holding him against his chest. Lilly felt her heart swell at the tender gesture and signalled for him to follow her to his bedroom. Gently placing him on his bed he stepped away for her to tuck him in, and as she placed a kiss on top of his head, Isla silently jumped up and settled herself beside him, as was their bedtime routine.

Creeping down the stairs, Lilly found her sitting room empty and all signs of the meeting gone. She realised that the room was in fact even tidier than it had been when everyone arrived, and she felt grateful at the kindness her new friends had shown her. Padding into the kitchen, she found Joel drying up the last of the dishes.

"Thank you, everywhere looks amazing," she gushed in gratitude. "And thank you for carrying Oliver to bed, he's getting heavier by the day!"

"He's a lovely little boy, a credit to you," replied Joel, and the look in his eyes told her that he meant it. She was standing barely three feet away from, and without dropping his gaze, he stepped forward, closing the gap between them. She felt her pulse quicken when he placed his arm around her and leaned into her. Lightly brushing his lips against hers, for only the briefest of moments, he then whispered, "Thank you for a lovely evening," before taking his leave with Katie, silently slipping out of her front door, into the darkness.

Bridget

Bridget felt a wave of anticipation flow through her as she pulled up outside of the quintessential village pub that Charles had chosen for their lunch date. She doubled checked her lipstick in her rear-view mirror, then barred her teeth to check for lipstick marks. She nodded to herself in the mirror. Her carefully applied make up was still ship-shape; it was time to go in and meet him.

With butterflies dancing in her stomach, she climbed out of her car and headed over to the pretty, flower-filled pub entrance. She saw him as soon as she walked through the door. He had chosen a table next to the window and she was touched that he remembered that window seats were always her favourite. He stood up as she approached and leaned forward to gently kiss her cheek in greeting.

"Hello Bridget," he said with a welcoming smile that made her butterflies switch from a gentle waltz to an up-tempo jive. *He gets more and more handsome each time I see him,* Bridget thought, as she slid into the chair opposite him.

After the usual pleasantries and small talk had been exchanged, Bridget moved the conversation on to the up-and-coming Rosewin fete. She was secretly thrilled to find Mr Parker to be very enthusiastic in offering his help in any way he could. And when he found out about the limited marketing and advertising experience among the Rosewin Rescue Fete team, he jumped at the chance to share the personal experiences he had used frequently for his own business, and even offered the expertise of his own marketing manager, Laura.

"I'll get her on to it straight away," Charles promised. "She is the best in the business, that lady can market anything and everything. The whole of Cornwall will know about your fete once Laura works her magic!"

Bridget was pleasantly surprised with his next comment.

"Are people allowed to visit the rescue centre?" he asked. "It would be great to see it for myself to get an idea of how to kick start the advertising campaign. This is something my company could be a part of for more than just the fete. My company could sponsor them in a professional capacity."

Bowled over by his enthusiasm and kindness, Bridget called Lilly to ask if she and Charles could pop in after lunch to discuss fundraising for Rosewin. Lilly, keen to raise as much money for her beloved charity as possible, assured her that they could visit whenever they liked.

Whilst sharing a delicious strawberry cheesecake for dessert, Charles confided that he was actually looking for a dog of his own. His weekend walks would be much more enjoyable with a furry friend by his side.

"Oh, what a wonderful idea," enthused Bridget. "I often take my little William for walks in the local woods, he is such great company and always keen to go exploring. But I hope you don't mind me saying," she said tentatively, "what about during the week when you're at work? From what Phoebe tells me you work very long hours. Might it be a little too long for him to be on his own?"

"That was my initial worry too," he admitted, but with a mischievous twinkle in his eye, he continued. "However, there are some perks to being the boss. I'll take the dog to work with me! We would both have constant companionship, and a lunch time walk would force me to get myself out of the office for a much needed half an hour break."

"Well then," beamed Bridget, "I think that sounds like the most splendid idea. Shall we go and see if the perfect dog for you is waiting at Rosewin as we speak?"

"My thoughts exactly," grinned Charles.

Lilly received them warmly when they arrived at Rosewin. "Welcome to Rosewin," she said, returning Bridget's affectionate hug and earnestly shaking hands with Charles. All the while, Milo stood beside her wagging his tail.

"And who's this?" enquired Charles. "One of the dogs in need of a home?" he asked, bending down to stroke Milo's silky soft ears.

"He's mine," Lilly proudly told him, "but he was one of our residents initially."

"He's a lovely chap," praised Charles, and Bridget could sense from his interaction with Milo that he truly was a dog lover and serious about his interest in rehoming a dog for himself. *Another wonderful thing about him* she thought. *A man's true character is always revealed by how he treats animals.*

Bridget couldn't keep the good news to herself any longer, "Lilly," she blurted out, "Charles is here to help with our fete! He owns the company where Phoebe works, and he's very generously offered his company's marketing expertise to help us get the fete advertised all over Cornwall!"

"Oh, my word, how amazing," replied Lilly, then Bridget quickly noticed she turned pale before continuing. "But how many more people are we talking? Do I need to hire another catering van? More wash facilities, do we need a bigger area?"

Bridget calmly placed her hand on Lilly's arm. "Absolutely nothing to panic about sweetheart. We still have just over two weeks to go, plenty of time to get everything sorted," she said soothingly. "Isn't that right Charles?"

Bridget was grateful when Charles replied, "There's more than enough time, don't you worry about a thing." He spoke in a calm, confident tone that she was sure he must use with his professional clients. No doubt that was one of the reasons he was so successful. Anyone investing large sums of money needed assurance that a confident, knowledgeable leader was at the helm to manage their interests.

She watched Lilly looking up at him, and she could see the panic ebbing away on hearing Charles's confidence.

"Thank you so much, I guess we'd better get started!" Lilly said to him. "Come over to my desk, I've got loads of ideas to share with you both."

Bridget listened quietly whilst Lilly updated Charles on the fundraising plans already set in motion and what was to be organised over the next two weeks. Bridget liked Lilly. Joel had explained all about Oliver to her, and her heart went out to them both. Bridget knew very well the heart-breaking realities of grief, but for a little boy to lose both of his parents at such a young age - even she couldn't imagine the colossal loss he had suffered. And for Lilly to lose her sister, her best friend, and somehow, she had managed to push through her own suffering and pain to raise her nephew as her own. Bridget thought she was a very special girl indeed.

During the fundraising meeting at Lilly's house, Bridget thought she had seen a little something between Lilly and Joel. Nothing concrete, just a feeling she sensed when they were together. And how Joel stepped in to carry little Oliver up to bed for her.

Yes, Bridget thought, *it would be wonderful if there was something growing between them.* Joel deserved someone lovely. He had been so focused on his career, so focused on providing for her and Phoebe after Jacob's death, so driven to earn and save in order to have enough money to put a deposit down on a property for him and Phoebe. It had been their dream since they were children. They had both always wanted the same thing, to wake up each morning and see their horses grazing in their own paddocks. And he had achieved it, they both had. She felt her heart swell with pride at how they had worked so very hard, together, in achieving their dream. But with all of his focus on work, it had left very little time for relationships. Bridget hoped that now he and Phoebe owned Pine Trees, he might be able to think about having someone to share it with, and Bridget got the feeling that Lilly and Oliver might be the very people he needed in his life.

"Bridget, Bridget, are you ok?" she heard Charles ask, with a concerned look on his face.

Pulling herself away from her daydreaming, she smiled up at him. "Yes, sorry, I was miles away!"

"Lilly has just offered for us to meet some of the residents. Apparently, there is a little West Highland White terrier that might be a good match for me. Would you like to come and see him with me?"

"Definitely," Bridget replied, "what's his name?"

"Rascal," Lilly laughed. "He's what you might call a bit of a character! But he loves people and provided he has a good walk in the morning, he should settle well at being an office dog. I think the communal aspect of the busy office will be perfect for his sociable personality."

Bridget and Charles followed Lilly through the back door of reception and down the corridor of kennels filled with barking, over-excited dogs.

So many dogs in need of a home, Bridget thought sadly as each dog tried to gain their attention as they walked past.

"Here he is," Lilly announced, stopping outside the kennel where a little white dog was bouncing up and down exuberantly. Lilly unlatched the door and gestured for Bridget and Charles to follow her inside.

After a mad thirty seconds of excitement from the little dog, he settled next to Charles and enjoyed being fussed by him quietly. "They are always crazy with excitement when someone visits them. It's a long, lonely day stuck in here, surrounded by the chaos of all the other dogs. All they want is attention and unfortunately with so many, the other staff and I just can't give them what they need. We usually find that once they are settled in their new home, they are much calmer, just like he is now."

Bridget could see how smitten Charles and Rascal where with each other. "He's a lovely dog, isn't he Charles?"

Charles didn't take his eyes off Rascal. "Yes, he is."

And Bridget could see the corners of his mouth breaking into a smile as the little dog rolled over for Charles to rub his belly.

Bridget caught Lilly's eye, and with a knowing look, she realised that Lilly was witnessing the same thing she was. Rascal and Charles were each other's match. She just knew it, just like she knew William was hers, the very first time she met him.

Joel

Joel pulled into Hollybrook stables, his last call of the day. He had received a message half an hour ago, asking if he could pop in on his way home, as one of the horses had lost a shoe and was due to compete tomorrow. Joel always prided himself on his excellent work ethic and reliability. It was one of the reasons he was highly sought after and so successful.

And one of the reasons I've never had time for a relationship! he thought ruefully. But he felt that area of his life was about to change. He was forty now, his business was thriving, his dream home had been purchased, and he was beginning to feel that it was time he found someone to share his life with. And Lilly was proving to be someone he wanted to spend as much of his time with as possible. Someone he looked forward to hearing from. His stomach did a somersault each time he saw her name flash up on his phone when a message beeped through.

Clare was waiting for him on the yard with Sundance, Hollybrook's golden showjumper.

"Thank you so much for calling in, Joel," Clare said, and he could hear the genuine gratitude in her voice.

"No problem at all, he'll have a full set of shoes on in no time!" replied Joel, stroking Sundance's neck before getting to work.

"I hear you're holding the fundraising fete for Rosewin at your place," Clare mentioned. "I'm so sorry we couldn't hold it here. Usually, I'd jump at the chance to help the rescue, but we are just chock-a-block with horses at the moment."

"Don't worry at all, hosting it at Pine Trees has motivated Phoebe and me to tidy the place up!" Secretly, he also thought that if the fete had been planned to be held at Hollybrook, then he wouldn't have been able to spend so much time with Lilly, so really, he was glad that Clare wasn't able to help out with a venue.

"The ladies and I want to do our bit though. Ellen will be bringing Pipsqueak and we'll all be baking homemade cakes for your mums' cake stall. From what I hear, the word is spreading far and wide, and your mum will need as many cakes as she can get!"

"Brilliant, thank you," he replied, grateful not only for her help and generosity, but also giving him an excuse to message Lilly and update her that they would not be short of cakes to sell on the day. Ever since the fundraising meeting at her house, Joel had found himself looking for any excuse to contact her.

After packing up his tools and finishing his cup of tea and slice of Victoria sponge cake, Joel said his goodbyes to Clare and climbed into his pick-up truck. His pulse skipped a beat as he dug out his phone and pinged a message off to Lilly about the Hollybrook ladies' cake donations. Just the thought of Lilly brought a smile to his face. Starting the ignition, he slowly trundled down the drive. Before he even reached the end of Hollybrook's driveway, his phone bleeped. Anticipation swept through him that it could be Lilly. He drew his truck to a halt and pulled out his phone and there it was, her name staring back at him on the screen.

Great news! The posters have arrived. Would you like to collect this evening? Or shall I give them to Phoebe tomorrow? Lilly

Joel had the idea of handing out posters to some of his clients. If there is one thing he had learnt about women and horses over the years, it was that they all love to help any animal in need. And he knew that ladies also had a habit of spreading the word! His large client base could bring in some much-needed visitors, along with their wallets, to the fete.

Joel typed his reply. *Just finished work. Passing your place in 10 mins. Could pop in and collect? Joel*

Joel would have to detour and take the long way home if he were to pass Lilly's home from Hollybrook, but there was no way he was going to miss out on an opportunity to see her! Another bleep.

See you in 10. Lilly

Joel hadn't actually seen her since their kiss last week. They had been exchanging messages daily, but all had been about the fundraiser. Joel secretly hoped that even once the fundraiser was over, he and Lilly would still be able to enjoy each other's company.

Joel knocked on her front door, and felt the usual fizzing inside him, knowing that she was now so very close to him, just on the other side of the door. He quickly tried to regain his composure as he heard the click of the door unlocking from the inside.

"Joel! Katie!" exclaimed Oliver. "Have you come for dinner? Aunty Lilly is just preparing it in the kitchen," said the little boy, taking hold of Joel's hand and dragging him inside.

"Hi Oliver," replied Joel, momentarily knocked off guard after mentally preparing himself to see Lilly, but instead having been greeted by a very enthusiastic Oliver.

"Aunt Lilly, Joel's here for dinner!" Oliver shouted out from the hallway, "Its spaghetti Bolognese, my favourite!" he said to Joel, before skipping off into the kitchen.

Joel felt somewhat flummoxed, and also slightly embarrassed by arriving at their dinner time. He hoped Lilly wouldn't think he had been presumptuous about dinner and expected to eat with them. He tentatively peered around the kitchen door.

"Hi Lilly," he stammered.

He was greeted with Lilly's beaming smile, "Hi Joel, you must be hungry after work, would you like to join us? I've made plenty."

"I don't want to impose, I didn't realise it was your dinner time," he admitted.

"Don't be silly! We'd love you to join us, wouldn't we Oliver?" Lilly replied enthusiastically.

"Yes, please stay Joel," Oliver said. He was already setting an extra place at their kitchen table.

Relaxing under their warm, friendly welcome, Joel replied, "Thank you, I love spaghetti!" And he was rewarded with two approving smiles.

The conversation flowed effortlessly between the three of them. Joel explained what he did for work to the two non-horsey listeners, both keen to understand a little more about his horsey world. Joel then listened intently as Oliver explained about his new topic at school. He was learning about King Henry VIII and was very keen to find out if Joel knew that Henry had chopped off the heads of two of his wives. Joel enjoyed the little boy's enthusiasm about the era of the Tudors. Lilly then moved the conversation on to her happy news. Little Rascal had officially been rehomed and left for his forever home with Mr Parker today.

Chatting in Lilly's cosy little kitchen, Joel realised that this is what he had been missing. Coming home to a family, sharing his day with people he cared about, and who cared about him. *But I wonder*, he thought, *would Lilly and Oliver want to be part of my family? Would they let me in to be a part of theirs?* It dawned on him that he would very much like evenings like this to be a regular occurrence.

After dinner Oliver asked to be excused so he could play outside with Milo and Katie, leaving Lilly and Joel alone in the kitchen. Helping Lilly tidy up, Joel filled the sink with hot, soapy water.

"I'll dry," Lilly said, and picking up her tea towel, she stepped towards him to stand at his side.

Focusing on the task at hand, Joel stared into the sink thinking, *this is my moment.*

"Dinner was delicious, thank you," he started, and before Lilly had chance to reply, or he lost his bottle, he continued. "Could I repay the favour?"

Lilly accepted the dripping plate from him and smiled when he caught her eye. "That sounds lovely, thank you."

"Are you free for a picnic lunch on Sunday?" Joel ploughed on, his confidence growing with her positive response.

"Oliver has a play date with a friend from school, but I'm free," she replied tentatively.

She's just as nervous as me, Joel noticed, secretly hoping that she was also feeling the warmth and affection growing between them.

"It's a date then," he said, "I'll pick you up at mid-day." And before they could say anymore, Milo and Katie came charging through the back door with Oliver hot on their heels.

"I'd better be heading home, the horses need to be fed. But thank you for a lovely evening," Joel said to Lilly as she handed him the box of posters for his clients.

"I'll see you on Sunday," replied Lilly, before reaching up on her tip toes and gently placing a kiss on his cheek.

Jack

In the solitude of his car, with the soft music of the radio playing, Jack was feeling tentatively hopeful that his friendship with Phoebe was slowly progressing into something more. Ever since he had given her the drawing, he felt that his feelings had been openly displayed to her. Such a detailed, intricate sketch could not have been created without the tender emotion an artist feels for his muse. And Phoebe's response showed a reciprocation of his own sentiments.

Work was still extremely busy, but they had managed to steal a few moments together; lingering looks, smiles across the office, and delicious pastries left as little surprises on each other's desks. They were at the tantalizing stage of unsaid words and emotion-filled pauses, coupled with nervous anticipation of what the other might be thinking.

Jack realised that he'd never looked forward to going to work so much. And the Rosewin rescue fete was the icing on the cake. An excuse to spend time with her away from the office.

Jack parked outside Rosewin and climbed out of his car. His Saturday afternoon was to be spent with Lilly and Phoebe, meeting all of the dogs and cats that were in desperate need of a forever home, and the subjects of his artwork for the fundraiser.

"Jack!" Phoebe called out, holding the rescue front door wide open. "We've been waiting for you. Come on in, I can't wait to meet all the animals!"

Jack smiled to himself as he swung the bag containing his camera and sketch pad over his shoulder, and replied, "I'm on my way!"

Phoebe's enthusiasm for anything related to animals was infectious. Her genuine affection just radiated out of her, and Jack couldn't help but be swept along with her. He liked animals, of course he did, but he was experiencing them in a whole new light through Phoebe. The connection she had with her own horse, her natural ability to communicate with Penelope, and animals in general, through trust and kindness, he found inspiring to watch. They were her true friends, and today, he would get to share the experience with her. He thought back to his first drawing of her - fairy girl, as Chloe had named her. And he felt he had captured her character perfectly, without even realising it at the time. Phoebe was a very pretty girl on the outside, but her inner goodness, tenderness and gentle nature was what he found truly captivating.

Phoebe ushered him inside.

"Jack, welcome to Rosewin," said Lilly, and Milo sat at his feet thumping his tail.

"Hi Lilly," he replied, before bending down to give Milo a gentle pat.

"I was just telling Phoebe about our new arrivals," explained Lilly. "I think I'd better take you straight through before she spontaneously combusts!"

"Puppies!" squeaked Phoebe.

Lilly burst into laughter before turning on her heel. "Come on, follow me. Let's put the poor girl out of her misery!"

Jack felt his heart skip a beat when Phoebe reached out and linked her arm through his.

"We're going to play with puppies!" she said excitedly.

Jack and Phoebe settled themselves on the kennel floor with Pixie, a non-descript black and white mixed breed dog, and her five adorable puppies.

"I'll leave you guys to it," said Lilly. "If I sit down with these little cuties, I'll never get any work done!" she chuckled, as she stepped outside of Pixie's kennel and closed the latch.

"All the dogs we have in at the moment are super friendly," she added. "You can let yourselves in to each kennel. Have fun!"

Pixie was a calm, attentive mother, and once the excitement of receiving visitors died down, she quietly snuggled up next to Jack whilst her puppies clambered over Phoebe. Jack took the camera out from his bag and began clicking away. He couldn't possibly sketch everyone today, so his idea was to take plenty of photographs of each animal so he could study them at home, and then his drawings could begin.

As Jack clicked away, he could tell that Phoebe was in her element. The five little puppies wriggled and squirmed all over her, each trying to gain her attention and affection. Her eyes shone with delight and her radiant smile was captured forever through his camera lens. He knew already that she would be etched into his sketchbook, along with the puppies, as a memory of this wonderful day with her.

"Aren't they just the most loveable munchkins!" giggled Phoebe. Then she cast her eyes over to Pixie. "I hope she finds her forever home too. Sometimes the older dogs get passed over in favour of a cute fluffy puppy," she said with a tinge of sadness in her voice.

Jack placed his camera down so he could give the quiet dog some attention. Her little tail wagged gently at the feel of his touch, and she let out a contented sigh once he fell into rhythmical strokes over her body. "She's a lovely natured girl, I'm sure she won't have a problem finding a new home," replied Jack.

Whilst Jack focused on Pixie, he heard a click, and on looking up, he saw that Phoebe had whipped out her phone to snap a picture of him and Pixie. "It's not fair that the puppies get all the attention," said Phoebe. "We need to make sure Pixie gets a new home too."

Jack noticed her brow furrow with concern at the thought of Pixie being pushed aside for one of her puppies. "Pixie will be my masterpiece, she will have a queue of people a mile long wanting to adopt her once they see her drawing at the fete," he said kindly.

"Let's switch places," he suggested, "so you can have a cuddle with Pixie?"

Nodding enthusiastically, Phoebe replied, "I'd like that, thank you Jack." And she carefully manoeuvred herself from underneath the pile of puppies to snuggle up with Pixie. Jack couldn't help but laugh at the antics the puppies got up to as they clambered about all over him, and each other, all the while Pixie slept contently, curled up beside Phoebe, with her head resting on Phoebe's lap. Jack watched her caress Pixie's ears as she snoozed.

"When Pine Tree's is eventually finished, and I can finally move into my own home, I'm going to get a dog," she told him. "And chickens! Fresh eggs every day, how great would that be?" Before he had chance to reply, she ploughed on. "And stable cats! Cats have a way of making a place feel homely, don't they?"

Jack could picture her in his mind's eye, stepping out of her back door to feed her friendly garden chickens, her little dog skipping along at her heels as she then headed over to the stables to look after her horses, while the stable cats snoozed amongst the hay bales. Pine Trees really would be her paradise home, and he wondered whether there would be room in her idyllic life for him and Chloe? Because it was very quickly dawning on him that he couldn't imagine his life without this enchanting girl in it.

Aloud, he said, "Absolutely, stable cats sound like the perfect addition to Pine Trees." Suddenly self-consciously concerned that she could read his thoughts, he blurted out, "We'd better say goodbye to Pixie and the pups, we have lots more dogs and cats to visit!"

The next two hours passed far too quickly for Jack, but the time had come for him to collect Chloe from her friend's house and as much as he didn't want to tear himself away from Phoebe, he couldn't leave his daughter waiting.

"I've got plenty of pictures to work from," he announced to Phoebe and Lilly." I'll get started as soon as I get home."

"Thank you so much, Jack," said Lilly. "Your drawings are definitely going to help some of our residents find their forever homes. And some much-needed pennies when they sell at the fete!"

"I'd better head off too, I've got to feed the horses," announced Phoebe, reaching towards Lilly for a brief goodbye hug. "Thank you for such a fantastic day!"

Waving goodbye to Lilly, Jack and Phoebe headed out of the door and walked side by side towards their cars. "I can't wait to see your drawings," said Phoebe, stepping towards him to give him a goodbye hug, just like she had Lilly.

Jack couldn't help himself, he returned her hug, and as he placed his arms around her, he held her to him for just a brief moment. She smelled of horses, and dogs, and since she was so very close to him, he could smell her light, lavender-scented perfume. He found the combination intoxicating, a very individual, personal fragrance to Phoebe. And he liked it very much.

He felt Phoebe relax into his arms. "I've had a wonderful day with you," he whispered.

"So have I, I've really enjoyed spending the day with you," replied Phoebe. "Now you must go and get Chloe!" And after reaching up to give him a gentle kiss on his cheek, she pulled away from him and walked over to her car. Climbing in, she gave him a warm, meaningful smile, before turning away and starting the ignition, and then she was gone.

Lilly

Lilly had just returned home after dropping Oliver off at his play date, and after catching sight of herself in the hallway mirror, she skipped up the stairs to try and make herself presentable for her date.

Date, she thought, *he definitely called it a date!* Butterflies fluttered around inside her with excitement.

Rummaging through her wardrobe, she pondered on what to wear. It wasn't a dinner date, so that ruled out dresses or skirts, which helped to narrow down her options. She couldn't wear her second favourite shirt again; he'd already seen her in that! Her dark denim jeans were clean on that morning, and were her most comfortable pair, with a strechy waist, which was always a good choice when going for a ramble in the woods. Flicking through her clothes she came across a baby pink coloured fitted shirt. It had been one of her favourites, but a mishap with a bramble bush when playing with Oliver last week had torn the bottom button off...*but tucked in with my navy-blue belt, no one would ever know! And it's ruined anyway so it won't matter if it gets dirty on the walk,* she decided, slipping it on and twirling in front of her mirror.

She brushed her wayward morning hair, then slicked it up into a ponytail, adding a smidge of lip-gloss to finish her look. Milo bounded into her bedroom, spinning in circles, then bounded back out and down the stairs. His exuberance alerted her that Joel had arrived. Just as she began to climb down the stairs herself, she heard a knock at her door. The dancing butterflies inside her fluttered more energetically at the thought of seeing him.

Opening her door, she saw not only Joel and Katie, but two ginormous horses. Her heartbeat quickened in mild panic as it quickly dawned on her that the picnic walk was not going to be on foot, but on horseback.

"Hello Joel," said Lilly, as her eyes darted between him and the horses.

"Hi Lilly," replied Joel, and picking up on her slightly apprehensive tone, he continued, "I thought you might like to ride Eliza again? She'll look after you," he told her, as he slowly ran his fingers over Eliza's nose. "She's the safest, smartest horse there is. I promise you can trust her," he finished, with a gentle smile.

"And who's this," Lilly asked, pointing at the large bay horse.

"This is Penelope, Phoebe's horse."

"And Phoebe doesn't mind you borrowing her on her day off?" enquired Lilly.

"She's gone riding on the moors with her friend Ellen today, and Ellen's boyfriend generously offered her his horse to ride, so she didn't mind me borrowing Pen for our picnic," he explained.

Lilly thought how kind Phoebe had been to her brother. She might not be horsey herself, but she knew that if someone had their own horse, loaning it out for someone else to ride was not done lightly, and she realised that Joel would have had to explain his reasons for borrowing Penelope. Since he was such a reserved man, it was clear to her that his intentions must be honest, if he'd shared his plan with Phoebe.

Acknowledging the effort Joel had gone to for their picnic and knowing that he would never put her in harm's way, the panic started to flow away, and a little fizzle of excitement started to bubble up inside her at the thought of going riding in the woods with Joel, and she had to admit to herself, that as far as first dates went, it was very romantic!

"Are you ready?" asked Joel.

"Definitely," replied Lilly, smiling broadly at him.

Joel held the stirrup for her. "Put your foot in there, and on my count of three, heave yourself up! I'll help you."

And when she heard him say "three," she felt his strong arms lift her up into to the air, and the next moment she was sitting in Eliza's saddle.

"Ok up there?" he asked, and after acknowledging her nod, he showed her how to hold the reins. "Or you can just hold on to her mane, I'll have her on the lead rope to keep you safe."

Eliza stood quietly whilst Lilly watched Joel put his foot in Penelope's stirrup and expertly swing his leg over in one fluid motion. *I doubt I looked that elegant getting on Eliza,* she thought ruefully. Turning Penelope around, he leaned forward and clipped a rope onto Eliza.

"Ready?" he asked.

After deciding that she would consider the reins a little bit further into the ride, once she'd got into the swing of things, Lilly clutched tightly onto Eliza's mane, smiled at Joel and said, "Ready!"

Eliza fell into a steady walk alongside Penelope, and as she began to get used to the gentle rhythm of Eliza walking beneath her, Lilly started to relax and enjoy the beautiful countryside scenery from horseback. Milo and Katie were skipping along beside them, and when they reached the entrance of the woods, the dogs galloped off after an enticing scent. They zoomed forwards and backwards, scouring the woodland for their quarry.

"I hear Phoebe had a fantastic day with you yesterday," said Joel.

"Oh yes," replied Lilly. "She had a brilliant day. Although it wasn't anything to do with me! It was more to do with the five adorable puppies that we have in at the moment."

"Yes, puppies will do it!" laughed Joel. "Animal bonkers she is! Rescuing some stable cats was casually dropped into conversation as well. No doubt planting the seed for when she canfinally move to Pine Trees and have space to rescue anything and everything that might need a home!"

There was silence between them for a while, then Joel asked, "And what do you think of Jack? I have a feeling that she's quite keen on him."

"I have a feeling Jack is quite keen on Phoebe!" replied Lilly. "I like him. He has a quiet, kind way with the animals, and you can tell a lot about a person with how they behave around animals. And he seems pretty smitten with Phoebe."

"I worry that sometimes she is too nice. She's so generous and thoughtful of others and lives in her own Phoebe world filled with rainbows and sunshine and Penelope. Sometimes I don't think she realises that not everyone is as kind as she is. Her last boyfriend was awful, walked all over her and then finished with her," he confided.

"It's never a bad thing to try and see the best in people," Lilly replied, "but I genuinely think you have nothing to worry about regarding Jack." And Lilly quietly thought how lucky Phoebe was to have such a caring big brother.

"This is it," announced Joel, "our picnic spot."

They had entered a little clearing in the middle of the woods with ample space for the horses to be tied up safely. The break in the trees presented them with a stunning view of the gentle river flowing between the valleys and hundreds of treetops far over on the other side. The sunshine speckled through the leaves, and with the heavy, musty scent of the pines, coupled with the gentle hum of the woodland creatures, Lilly felt like she had entered an enchanted woodland, like that of a fairy tale.

"It's beautiful here, Joel. I've walked through these woods nearly every day since I moved here and have never come across this place," said Lilly.

"That's why we brought the horses!" he replied. "We can cover a lot more ground with them than on our own two feet. Eliza and I come here quite often;

we've never seen another person here." And with a shy smile, he continued, "Other than Eliza, you're the first person I have brought here."

Lilly watched Joel dismount from Penelope, rummage around in his saddlebag, and produce her headcollar. Unbridling her, he slipped on her headcollar and securely tied her to a branch. Turning to Lilly, he asked, "Would you like me to help you down?"

"Yes please," she replied.

"Take your feet out of the stirrups," he said, as he walked over to her and Eliza. Standing next to Eliza, he looked up at her. "Now lean over and put your hands on my shoulders."

Lilly quietly did what Joel asked, and once her hands were resting on his shoulders, he slid his hands under her arms and carefully lifted her down. Sandwiched between Joel and Eliza, Lilly could feel the warmth emanating from them both, and smell the sweet horsey aroma coupled with Joel's musky aftershave. Joel didn't step back. Instead, he silently lifted his hand and gently traced her jawline with his finger. Lilly felt her pulse quicken as he tentatively leaned towards her and softly brushed his lips with hers. Lingering for just a moment, he then slowly pulled away from her. He slipped his arms around her and held her close to him, then after planting an affectionate kiss on her cheek, he announced, "Picnic time!"

Settled side by side on Joel's green tartan picnic rug, tucking into ham sandwiches, blueberry muffins and flask of tea, with Milo and Katie snoozing at their feet, Joel asked, "How are the fundraiser preparations coming along? Only one more week to go!"

"I know," replied Lilly. "The past three weeks have flown by. But everyone has been so kind and helpful, and Laura, Mr Parker's marketing manager, has been amazing. She's even managed to get it advertised over the local radio station! Thank you so much for letting us hold it at Pine Trees, we couldn't have done any of this without you," said Lilly, slowly slipping her hand into his.

Joel linked his fingers through hers, and she could feel the masculine roughness of his hands. Turning to face her, smiling at her with his twinkling eyes, he said, "I'm happy to have been able to help."

Lilly rested her head on his shoulder, drank in the spectacular view, then closed her eyes. She wanted to remember this moment forever. A perfect moment in time captured, when for once, she didn't feel the heavy burden of raising Oliver on her own. She didn't feel the aching grief for her beloved sister. She didn't feel all alone in the world. All she felt, at that moment in time, was peace and contentment, with Joel.

Bridget

Bridget placed the last cherry on top of the final batch of iced cupcakes.

Finished! She cast her eyes over the hundreds of tasty cakes and treats laid out on her kitchen table that she had created over the previous two days.

Phoebe had been up at the crack of dawn to feed the horses and run her own errands before the fete began at ten o' clock. Joel had two morning clients to see but he had assured them that he would be ready for his car parking duties in plenty of time. And Bridget had spent the early morning hours baking and icing the last three batches of cupcakes.

Bridget's doorbell rang out clearly in the quiet house. She checked the clock on the kitchen wall.

"Eight thirty, and I'm not even ready yet!" Bridget mumbled to herself. Dusting icing sugar off her red checked apron, she opened her front door to greet Charles and a very enthusiastic Rascal.

"Good morning, Bridget," said Charles.

"Charles, hello, come on in," welcomed Bridget, holding her door wide open and ushering him in. "Rascal, come on into the kitchen, I've got a treat for you!" And the little dog trotted along with her before bursting into excitement overdrive when she produced a sausage for him.

"Wow," exclaimed Charles, "you have been busy. Should I start loading the car up?" Charles gestured to the piles of cake-filled Tupperware boxes on the table.

"Wonderful, thank you, I'll just nip upstairs and freshen up," replied Bridget.

After being alone for so many years, Bridget found herself welcoming Charles's help and kindness, and company. She'd forgotten what it was like to share things with someone. Of course, she had Joel and Phoebe, but they had their own lives to lead. She looked forward to his messages, which were now a daily occurrence, and she felt that their relationship was beginning to blossom.

Both she and Charles had decided that she should discuss their budding situation with Phoebe and Joel after the fete. She didn't want any distractions for them before the big day, but once calm was restored, and everything got back to normal she would sit them down and explain everything to them. She worried that it might rock the boat somehow for Phoebe, with Charles being her boss. But Charles had assured her that work was just that, work. And when he was in the office, with Phoebe, everything would be just as usual. Bridget was his private life, and he and Phoebe were both very capable of keeping it separate.

Deep down Bridget hoped that her children would be happy for her. *I'm sure they will be,* she thought, *Mr Parker is a lovely man, and I know they would want me to be happy. One more day to go, and then I can tell them everything.* Bridget knew she would feel much better once hers and Charles's courtship was out in the open.

After a quick change into the freshly pressed dress she'd picked out the night before, and a squirt of her favourite perfume, she hurried down the stairs to help Charles finish packing up the car.

By midday the Rosewin rescue fete was in full swing. The temperamental British weather blessed them with warm sunshine and a light fluttering of gentle breeze.

It was just perfect. From where she was positioned behind the cake stall table, Bridget could hear the squeals and laughter from the children on the bouncy castle and the hubbub of happy, contented fete goers. There was a sense of joyful merriment filling the air.

Bridget watched Clare and Suzie approaching, both of whom were laden down with boxes filled with cakes which Bridget was grateful to see due to her own stocks diminishing much more quickly than she anticipated.

She introduced Charles and Rascal to the Hollybrook ladies. "I'm lucky to have two such enthusiastic helpers for the day," she smiled. "Charles, Clare and Suzie are some of Joel's clients from Hollybrook stables."

"Great to meet you, and to see a successful rescue!" said Clare.

"What a brilliant day this is turning out to be!" gushed Suzie. "Hopefully all these people are spending money and Rosewin will receive a hefty donation by the end of it!" And after she placed her boxes down, she rummaged around in her purse and produced a pound. Handing it over to Bridget, "I've heard your cinnamon buns are legendary! I'll take one please before they run out."

"We've come to take our turn manning the cake stall, so you two can have an hour or so to grab some lunch and enjoy the fete," announced Clare.

Handing Suzie her bun, Bridget replied, "Wonderful, thank you." Grabbing her handbag, she linked her arm through Charles's, and with Rascal skipping along beside them, they set off to enjoy the fete and check how their friends were getting on with their own fundraising stalls.

She spotted Lilly first, clipboard in hand, talking into her radio with the other, whilst waiting in the queue at the hot dog stand.

"Lilly, hi," called out Bridget, making her way, with Charles at her side, through the throng of people to get to her.

"Bridget!" greeted Lilly. "I can't believe how busy it is. That was Joel on the radio. Cars are still streaming in and have been since ten o' clock this morning. He's starving! He's got no chance of getting away from his car parking duties, so I promised I'd take him a hot dog!"

Bridget laughed, and replied, "He's always hungry, I'd take him two hot dogs if I were you!"

"What a turn out," said Charles. "You really have done yourself, and the rescue centre proud."

Bridget noticed Lilly blush under his praise.

"It wasn't just me; everyone has helped me enormously. And I couldn't have done it without Joel's generosity of allowing the fete to be held at Pine Trees," she shyly replied.

"Now don't you be modest," chipped in Bridget. "You have been the driving force behind it all. Joel is happy to help, we all are. And Rose and Andrew will be thrilled with what you have achieved."

"They were so disappointed not to have been able to come today, but they had a phone call last night about three neglected donkeys, so they were off first thing this morning to rescue them. Their work never ends," replied Lilly ruefully.

"And that is what this is all about. The money you have raised today will do wonders for so many animals in need," said Bridget, giving Lilly an affectionate squeeze on her arm. All the while she was thinking how perfect Joel and Lilly were for each other. She hoped that they both knew it, or would come to realise it very soon.

Bridget and Charles said their goodbyes to Lilly and casually strolled through the fete, soaking up the bustling atmosphere.

"Let's go and see Phoebe and William," suggested Bridget. "I'm sure the pony petting will be popular."

And Bridget was right. A queue of children, with equally keen parents, were waiting patiently for their turn to pet the two adorable little ponies. She saw them munching on their hay nets, revelling in the adoration the children were bestowing upon them.

"William will be in his element!" giggled Bridget. "He just loves to be fussed and cuddled."

When they arrived, Ellen was looking somewhat frazzled.

"Hi Ellen," said Bridget, "you look busy!"

"Bridget, hello. Gosh, yes. I've had a constant stream of people keen to meet the ponies since we opened. And I'm on my own! Phoebe still hasn't turned up. Do you know what time she's arriving? I could really do with some help here!"

"Phoebe's not here?" enquired Bridget. "She told me she would be here by nine thirty to help you get the ponies organised before the fete started."

"Yep, that's what she told me," replied Ellen. "But when I arrived William was all prepared, waiting in his stable, and Phoebe was nowhere to be seen."

"She did have to pop into town this morning, I wonder if she got delayed?" questioned Bridget. "I'm sure she'll be here soon. I'll give her a quick call."

"Thanks, although I've been calling her all morning and her phone just rings out," explained Ellen.

Bridget rummaged around in her handbag for her phone, and then it slowly dawned on her that her phone was not in her bag. She had been in such a rush this morning, she had left it charging on the kitchen counter. She began to feel a knot of panic forming in the pit of her stomach.

No need to worry, she firmly told herself. *I'm sure there is a perfectly reasonable explanation.*

"What if I stay and give Ellen a hand," suggested Charles calmly, "and you go and find Jack. Phoebe was very keen to see his drawings of the animals, maybe she has just got waylaid at his stall."

Bridget felt herself begin to relax after hearing Charles's very feasible explanation. She had definitely sensed a glimmer of something between the two of them when they were at Lilly's house. It was perfectly normal that she might have been side-tracked by her desire to be in Jack's company.

"Good idea, thank you Charles," replied Bridget.

Bridget knew as soon as she spotted Jack's stall that Phoebe was not with him. She recognised Jack straight away, but the slight female figure standing beside him was most definitely not Phoebe. On nearing, she realised she must be Chloe, Jack's teenage daughter.*Stay calm,* she thought, *no need to raise the alarm yet. Maybe I've just missed her, and she is on her way to Ellen right now.*

"Hello, Jack," Bridget said with as much cheerfulness as she could muster.

"Hello Bridget," replied Jack, and instantly turned to Chloe. "This is Bridget, Phoebe's mum, and Bridget, this is my daughter, Chloe." Bridget could sense the pride in his voice as he introduced his daughter.

"What a pleasure to meet you," Bridget said kindly to the girl, and was rewarded with a shy smile in return.

"I can't wait to meet her," Chloe said quietly. "I've heard so much about her."

Bridget fleetingly thought that she wished her mind wasn't so occupied with where Phoebe was, so she could sit down and get to know both Chole and Jack. Chloe seemed to be such a lovely girl. But concern overtook such ideas. "She hasn't been over to see you yet?" enquired Bridget.

"Not yet, but I'm sure she's just busy with the ponies. No doubt we'll meet up with her at the end of the day," replied Jack.

Uneasiness swept over Bridget on learning that Jack and Chloe had not seen Phoebe either.

"You haven't seen or heard from her all day?" Bridget probed.

"I received a message first thing this morning saying she was looking forward to seeing my drawings and meeting Chloe at some point today," replied Jack.

Her anxiety was becoming more difficult to conceal. Jack must have sensed something wasn't quite as it should be, and he continued, "Is everything ok Bridget?"

She noticed concerned looks flicker between father and daughter before he settled his eyes back on her.

In a quiet voice, Bridget replied, "I'm not sure. No one seems to have seen her all day. I've foolishly left my phone at home and have no way to contact her."

Jack immediately pulled his phone out of his pocket and handed it to her. "Here, you can use mine, why don't you try her now," he said kindly.

The phone rang, and rang, and rang. "No answer," said Bridget, the panic no longer hidden in her voice. "Where on earth can she be?"

Phoebe

Phoebe woke up at four o' clock in the morning, bright eyed and bushy tailed. It was futile for her to try and go back to sleep - she was far too excited about the day ahead. Not only was it Rosewin's fete, but she was finally going to meet Chloe. She felt that Jack would not have encouraged their meeting if he was not serious about the growing feelings and budding relationship between them. And she couldn't wait to give him his gift. After receiving the beautiful, heartfelt drawing of her and Isabella, Phoebe wanted to repay his kindness. The picture she had captured of Jack and Pixie was perfect, even if she did say so herself! Although she didn't consider herself to be particularly artistic, she could clearly see how the camera had captured the tender moment between man and dog flawlessly. She would be collecting the enlarged, framed print from the photograph shop as soon as it opened at nine o'clock this morning. She couldn't wait for Jack to see it!

Tip toeing down the stairs, she padded into the kitchen to fill her flask with tea, and on seeing her mother's cinnamon buns all boxed up ready for the fete, she opened the lid and breathed in the delicious smell. *Hmmmm my favourite! Mum won't notice one missing,* she thought, delving into the box for a tasty breakfast treat. Scribbling a note for her mum explaining she would meet her at the fete later, she stepped out of her front door into the misty morning air.

Phoebe could feel the warmth of Penelope's breath on her fingers as she slipped the bit into her mouth. Tightening up her girth, she slid her foot into the stirrup and effortlessly mounted her horse. Affectionately running her fingers under her mane, and giving her withers a gentle scratch, she leaned forward and breathed in Penelope's sweet horsey scent.

It was now half past five and an orange glow was pushing through the dusky air to signal that the morning sun was beginning to rise. Surrounded by the silence of dawn, Phoebe breathed in deeply, squeezed her legs gently, and quietly said, "Come along now girl, let's go riding."

Being alone amongst the pine trees sent shivers down her spine and brought tingles to her skin. Not of fear, but excitement. The empty woodland cast shadows as the sun's golden droplets began to trickle through the dense forest firs, to burn away the morning mist. Listening to the sound of Penelope's steady hoofbeats beneath her, engulfed in the mystical woodland glow, Phoebe felt alive. There was something about riding, being atop a fellow sentient creature, that made her connection with nature feel that much deeper. It was a closeness that drew her inner being to the forefront of all the natural beauty that was around her. An appreciation for her majestic horse, the curious woodland creatures, and the flora and fauna that managed to survive under the gloom of the pine trees. A knowledge of the tender, and somewhat fragile connection between all earthly beings. And above all, she felt at peace.

"You like him, don't you Pen?" Phoebe asked her horse.

She watched Penelope twitch her ears in reply.

"Good," she said, smiling down at her. "I thought you did; I mean who wouldn't!" she gushed. And she acknowledged more ear twitches from her friend, to show that Penelope was indeed fully participating in the conversation and definitely as keen on Jack as she was. "I'm meeting Chloe today," she continued, as Penelope plodded along the narrow track, carefully stepping over fallen branches and tree roots. Holding complete trust in Penelope to navigate the undulating surface beneath her, Phoebe admitted, "I'm a little nervous. What if she doesn't like me? What if we don't get along. How can I have a relationship with Jack if Chloe isn't ok with it?"

Phoebe heard Penelope offer her deep, throaty nicker. It was a sound very rarely offered unless important information was being discussed between them. Phoebe felt her worries melt away as she interpreted her loyal friend's whispers - *of course she will like you! Plus, you always have me!*

"You are absolutely right, as always Pen!" Phoebe said aloud to her horse. And as the track began to open out, she could feel Penelope building beneath her, asking her politely if they could go running. Phoebe offered her a loose reign, and with a gentle squeeze with her legs, Penelope trotted purposely for three strides before breaking out into a fast, exhilarating canter. Phoebe could feel all of her concerns swirling away as she focused only in the moment. It was just her and Pen, alone in the alluring forest, galloping as one.

Fully refreshed from her early morning ride, Phoebe kissed Penelope on her velvety soft nose, and said her goodbyes. Climbing into her car, she started the ignition, and anticipation for the day ahead swept through her.

Bumbling along the country lanes, Phoebe headed towards the local town. Her mind filled with the possibilities of what might be to come if all went well when she met Chloe. *Does she like horses?* she wondered; *I would love for her to meet Pen! I could teach her to ride. How exciting would that be!* And her thoughts drifted to her horse, her beautiful, wonderful friend, Penelope. And Jack. *How romantic would it be if we went riding together? Picnicking in the woods like Joel and Lilly did the other day!* She then began to wonder what it might be like to kiss him. There had been several moments, moments when she was in such close proximity to him that she could feel his warm breath on her neck. So close that she could smell the subtle scent of his after shave. It was enough to make her feel giddy! She found herself filled with passionate anticipation of what it might feel like for him to gently brush his lips against hers.

That car is going too fast, was the first conscious thought that penetrated Phoebe's thoughts, and in a split second brought her mind hurtling back into the present. Claustrophobia engulfed her as she sensed the large Cornish hedges shrouding her. Only a moment ago, they had filled her with such joy as she had watched the pretty hedgerow flowers dancing in the light breeze. But now, the tall, broad hedges gave her nowhere to go. They trapped her on the narrow country lane. Fear ricocheted through her as she realised in horror that there was nothing she could do. It happened so fast. The speeding car flew around the blind corner with such power, the impact was instantaneous.

Phoebe felt the sudden, unavoidable collision and her little car crumbled under the brute strength of the oncoming vehicle. The noises surrounding her were deafening. The screech of rubber tyres skidding, the crunching of metal imploding, and the rapid beat of her own pulse thumping in her ears. Pain shot through her trembling body as it jerked with force from the impact of the two cars colliding and crashing to a halt.

Joel

Joel watched Lilly walk away from him. His eyes never left her slight frame as she elegantly strolled across the car parking field. He held his breath, and there it was. She stopped and turned to smile, and her eyes twinkled right at him, before she disappeared behind the hedge, making her way back to the fete. Joel felt himself glow on the inside from receiving her intimate glance, a look bestowed only on him.

Feeling fully replenished from his two hotdogs, an apple pastry, and a glass of refreshing lemonade that Lilly had kindly delivered too him, he ambled over to the other side of the field to greet the next customer. He felt a lightness in him that he hadn't felt in a very long time, a sense of excitement for the future unfolding before him. His beloved Pine Trees was slowly taking shape as each day passed. As the weeks ticked by, his ramshackle farmhouse was slowing transforming into his forever home. And Lilly. He knew, without a shadow of a doubt, that Lilly was becoming the most important person in his life, as well as little Oliver, and the future was something that they could share together.

The loud shrill ring of his mobile phone brought him away from his daydreaming.

"Hello. Is that Joel?" asked an unknown questioning voice. "A Mr Joel Fellows?"

"Yes, speaking," he casually replied, unperturbed to receive a call from an unknown person. It was a regular occurrence when potential new clients contacted him.

"Phoebe Fellows' brother?" the voice continued.

Phoebe? he thought, momentarily confused, *why would a customer want to discuss Phoebe?*

Aloud, he said, "Yes, I'm Phoebe's brother."

He heard a slight intake of breath before the unknown caller finally revealed themselves. "I'm Doctor Roberts, calling from Truro hospital."

Joel felt himself stiffen on hearing the words 'doctor' and 'hospital'.

The doctor continued, "I've been trying to contact Mrs Bridget Fellows, your mother, but unfortunately I haven't been able to get hold of her. Phoebe has been in a serious accident. She was brought to the hospital via ambulance this morning."

Joel's world stopped. He tried to process what the doctor was telling him. All he could stutter in response was, "She's in hospital?"

"Yes," replied the doctor calmly. "I strongly suggest you and your mother get here as soon as you can."

"Thank you, Doctor," Joel said, before hanging up the phone and staring blankly into space. He couldn't take in the magnitude of what the doctor had just told him. After a brief pause to gather his thoughts, the panic kicked in. *Oh holy Jesus, Phoebe's in hospital.*

He broke out into a sprint. Tearing across the carpark, he skidded through the gate way, then continued running full pelt down into the bustling fete. His mind was whirling in fear and anxiety, and the higgledy-piggledy lay out of the fete stalls, colourfully strewn over his paddock, made him momentarily disorientated. He paused, trying to get his bearings.

The cake stall, he thought. *Mum will be there.* Feeling more purposeful, he navigated his way through the bustling throng of laughing families, weaved between the many homemade crafts and games stalls, before finally setting eyes on the table, adorned with the familiar red and white checked tablecloth belonging to his mother, groaning under the weight of the many delicious treats on display for sale.

He saw his mother standing behind the table, deep in conversation with Mr Parker, an anxious expression etched on her brow. He momentarily slowed, to prepare himself for the devastating news he was about to share with her. He knew, once it had been said, and it was out in the open, the wheels would be set in motion for what they would undoubtedly face once they arrived at the hospital. The doctor had been vague, but from the grave tone of his voice, and the importance for he and his mother to get to the hospital as soon as possible, he knew Phoebe must be in a very bad way. And now he must tell his mother.

"Joel," Bridget called out.

She had spotted him; he could delay the inevitable no longer. "Mum," he replied loudly, in an effort to be heard over the noisy crowds, and swiftly covered the short space between them. He did not want to cause concern to any of the fete goers. The fete must be successful for raising the money the rescue centre so desperately needed, and he didn't want to cause ripples of worry amongst the people who were there to have a good time. He did not know for sure what was going on and sweeping speculations coupled with frivolous gossip were definitely not what his mother needed right now.

Standing directly between Bridget and Charles, he lowered his voice for only them to hear him. In an effort to convey enough information to ensure his mother hurried, but not enough to cause her blind panic, he settled on the words, "Mum, we need to go now. I'll explain everything on the way. It's to do with Phoebe."

Concern flooded her eyes as she questioned him. "I've been looking for her for ages. No one has seen her since this morning. Is she alright? Has something happened to her? What's going on?"

She spoke so quickly that Joel couldn't reply, even if he had wanted too.

"And what about the cakes?" Bridget gestured towards the queue of people beginning to form on the other side of the table.

Charles gave Joel a knowing look. A look that told Joel that he knew it was for the best that whatever it was he needed to discuss with his mother, it should be done in private.

"Don't you worry about a thing, Charles said. "I'll stay here and take care of the cakes. You go off with Joel. I'll catch up with you later." And with an affectionate pat on her arm, he turned to the waiting customer. "Beautiful day, isn't it. What can I get for you?"

Joel was grateful for Charles's proficiency and discretion. He gathered up his mother's handbag, linked his arm through hers, and said, "Come along now Mum, we've got to go." He escorted her through the crowd, across the neighbouring paddock, and all the way down to his pick-up truck, parked securely on the yard, tucked out of the way.

Joel drove as close to the speed limit as he could muster, trying to quell the fear rippling through him as he focused on the road ahead of him.

"Tell me again, exactly what the doctor said," asked Bridget. The distress was clearly audible in her voice.

"I've told you everything he said. She was in an accident this morning and taken to hospital by ambulance. I promise you Mum, that's all I Know," replied Joel. He was trying to remain calm for his mother. Her panic was rapidly rising as each minute passed and he knew that one of them had to keep it together, at least on the outside. On the inside, he was just as frighted as is mother about what they would have to face when they reached the hospital.

Finally pulling into the hospital carpark, Joel looked at his mother, clasping his hand in hers, he said, "Are you ready?"

Gripping his hand tightly, she nodded. Together, walking arm in arm, they made their way to the hospital reception desk.

"She's alive," was the first thing Doctor Roberts told them after he had introduced himself. "But I'm going to be honest with you, she's in a bad way."

Joel heard a sharp intake of breath from his mother as she tightened the grip she had on his arm. Placing his hand over his mother's to offer her some comfort, he nodded at the doctor to continue.

"She was in a head on collision with a speeding car, and the fierce impact caused an explosion. I'm afraid Phoebe has been severely burned."

"Can, can I see her, " stammered his mother in reply.

"Yes, of course you can, follow me. She's awake, but slightly confused and still trying to process everything that has happened to her, " warned the doctor. "And she's been given a lot of medication for the pain, don't expect too much," he cautioned.

Joel held back as he and Bridget stepped inside Phoebe's private hospital room. Shock and horror pumped through his veins when he saw her. Her face was bruised, her left cheek and top lip looking twice the size they should, and she was bandaged from the neck all the way down her left arm, torso and left knee. *That must be where she has been burned,* he thought. Bile rose to the back of his throat as the magnitude of what had happened to her was revealed before him. After the constant stream of nervous energy his mother had emitted since hearing of the accident, in the confines of Phoebe's small room, now she was the epitome of calm. She went straight to Phoebe, held her right hand in hers, and gently said her name.

"Phoebe, it's Mum, I'm here now. Everything is going to be ok, love. Don't you worry about a thing."

Phoebe opened her eyes to the sound of her mother's voice. "Mum," she whispered, before closing her eyes and drifting back off into her drug-induced sleep.

Joel felt tears spring to his eyes and an overwhelming wave of helplessness engulfed him. He stood, rooted to the spot, struggling to take in what had happened to his little sister, and the thought of how the terrible injuries she had suffered would affect her future.

His mother turned to him, and gently raised her hand to beckon him over. She placed her arm around him and held him to her. "Everything is going to be alright, Joel, it has to be. We got through losing your father, and we are going to get through this, together, I promise."

With the comfort of his mother's arm around him, in a somewhat awkward stance for a tall broad man, against a petite, genteel woman, he rested his head on her shoulder. She was his mother, and feeling the impact of her soothing words, he allowed his tears to spill. *I will be strong for both of them when Phoebe wakes up,* he thought determinedly. But right now, the overwhelming happenings of the day were too much for him. In the private, quiet hospital room, Joel and Bridget silently wept.

Jack

Slumped on his sofa, his untouched morning coffee cup clasped between his hands, Jack was feeling thoroughly perplexed. It had been one week since Phoebe's accident, and he hadn't been able to see her. Initially, it was family visiting only. *Of course it was, that's the way it should be,* he told himself. He understood that.

But it made him question the exact nature of his relationship with Phoebe. So many things had been left unsaid between them. He knew they were friends, that much he was sure of, but was she his girlfriend? That question was still up in the air.

He wanted her to be, desperately, and he had presumed that after she and Chloe had met, that things would then be able to progress. They were still at the very beginning stages of what he hoped was heading in the direction to being more than friends, but they were not there yet. And that was the crux of his predicament.

How much did Bridget know? What had Phoebe told Joel? He got the feeling that Phoebe was open and honest with her family, but to what extent about her feelings towards him, he was unsure. He couldn't just waltz into the hospital and claim to be her boyfriend in order to see her, no matter how much he wanted to. He had spent the last week waiting patiently for updates from Bridget. Her daily messages told him that she understood that there was something between him and Phoebe, but it wasn't quite clear what she thought, beyond that. And he was eternally grateful for her updates; they at least gave him some comfort.

However, after his initial request that he might be able to visit her, the day after her accident, was politely refused for the time being, he knew it was best not to push the matter, and now felt he was in limbo, waiting to be invited. And every time he received another message from Bridget, he waited for an invitation to be offered, but it never came, to his constant disappointment.

His heart broke at the thought of not being able to comfort Phoebe, at not being able to hold her in his arms and tell her that he would be by her side, no matter what. That he would care for her during her recovery. And that he loved her. That he had been drawn to her the first time he saw her splayed out on the office floor. He had fallen in love with her as he watched her riding Issy, and had continued to fall head over heels in love with her the more she shared her unique and wonderful personality with him. He had never met anyone like her. She held him under her warm, captivating spell.

"Why don't you leave someflowers at the hospital reception?" Chloe suggested.

"I don't want to seem as if I'm imposing, when they've made it clear that for the time being they're considering this to be a family matter," he replied, trying to keep the frustration of the whole situation out of his voice.

Chloe was innocent to the fact that ever since Phoebe's accident, he had been buried under an avalanche of self-loathing. The guilt swarmed through his veins for not being there when she needed him the most. He had categorically failed to protect her, and for that, he could not forgive himself.

It wasn't Chloe's fault, and he was going to try his damndest not to take his own pain out on her. She had been a rock by his side ever since they both learned of the accident, and he would not fail her like he had failed Phoebe. He softened his expression towards her, but before he had chance to reply, she continued.

"But you wouldn't be imposing," she pushed. "You're not going to visit her; you could just drop off some flowers with a card to let her know you're thinking of her. If it were me, I'd want to know that someone was thinking of me, even if I wasn't up for visitors."

Jack looked at his daughter. *When you put it like that,* he mused, *it wouldn't be going against Bridget's wishes. Anyone would send flowers in a situation like this surely? And if it would make Chloe happy...*

"Plus, " Chloe truthfully announced, "you've been moping around the house all week, it's time to do something proactive, don't you think? You'll feel better afterwards, I'm sure of It," she said with that knowing teenage look of hers.

How did she get so wise and worldly? he thought, proud of the young lady she was becoming.

Jack read and re-read the note for the twentieth time.

Dear Phoebe, I'm thinking of you, and I'm here for you. Anything you might need, please don't hesitate to call me. Jack x

Oh for god's sake, stop over thinking it! He chastised himself, finally sliding it into the little envelope. And before he could change his mind, he picked up the bouquet of fresh pink tulips, soft cream roses and lightly fragranced lavender flowers. He had carefully chosen the selection himself at the florist near his home. With a purposeful walk, he strolled into the hospital. His courage did not let him down, and after a brief exchange with the very friendly receptionist, who assured him his bouquet would be delivered to Phoebe, he was back outside in less than five minutes. Relief flooded through him. *Chloe was right! I do feel better for having done something productive.*

"Jack!"

Jack turned around at the sound of his name being called.

"Jack, hi, I thought it was you," said Joel, walking over to him.

Jack felt himself colour with embarrassment at having been spotted by Joel, after Bridget had explicitly said Phoebe was not up to visitors.

"I only dropped some flowers off for her," he stammered. "I'm not here to see her."

Joel smiled kindly at him, and he felt himself begin to relax when he realised Joel was not there to chastise him.

"How kind of you, Phoebe lovesflowers," replied Joel.

A slightly awkward silence fell between them, now that they had exchanged pleasantries, and not really knowing one another, the two men quietly stood side by side in the hospital car park.

"Are you busy?" Joel blurted out.

Jack had been decidedly unbusy ever since Phoebe's accident. His schedule for the foreseeable future was completely empty whilst he awaited his invitation to see Phoebe.

"No, not really," Jack carefully replied.

Joel pointed in the direction of where his pickup truck was parked, "That's mine. Follow me."

Jack acknowledged his gesture with a nod, and curious to see where this sudden invitation to spend time with Phoebe's brother might lead, he replied simply, "Ok."

Jack followed Joel's pick-up truck all the way to Pine Trees. He watched Joel park up, stroll over to the yard, and disappear inside the tack room, before reappearing with two head collars. Jack slowly climbed out of his car and hesitantly walk over to the yard.

"Wait here," instructed Joel, then he strode over to the closest paddock where the three horses were quietly grazing. In what seemed like no time at all, he returned with Penelope and Eliza. Securely tying them up outside their stables, he handed Jack a grooming brush and pointed at Eliza.

The silence was almost deafening. He had so many questions he wanted to ask

Joel about Phoebe, going round and round in his head, but nothing came out. And he felt that Joel's quiet, calm demeanour implied that he was not ready to talk just yet. Still bewildered at the turn of events, and to find himself standing on Pine Trees yard, without Phoebe, Jack set about brushing Eliza, just like she taught him. As he repeated the long rhythmical strokes over her enormous body, he felt her relax under his attention. She cocked her back leg, closed her eyes, and sighed gently. The repetitive motion began to calm his spinning mind as he focused on the task at hand.

Joel finally broke the silence between them, "If in doubt, go riding. That has always been mine and Phoebe's motto. In our world, horses fix everything."

Jack felt that Joel's words were a statement which didn't need reply, especially as he did not belong in the world of horses like Phoebe and Joel, and so he simply nodded and continued to groom Eliza.

Joel appeared next to him, a saddle over his arm, and as Jack stepped back to make room, he swung it up and onto Eliza's broad back. *It looks like I'll be going riding then,* thought Jack. Although only having ridden once before at the work team building weekend, he felt no anxiety about stepping back into the saddle. Eliza appeared strong and calm, and Joel had the same sense of capability and reassuring nature that Phoebe had around horses. Plus, being in the company of Eliza and Penelope made him feel closer to Phoebe.

Sitting on Eliza, Jack leaned forward and stroked the beautiful grey horse's mane.

"Eliza is as safe as they come, " said Joel, as he placed his foot in Penelope's stirrup and swung himself up and into her saddle. "She'll follow quietly wherever Penelope and I go. Phoebe told me the work weekend was the first time you'd ever ridden a horse. No need to worry about a thing."

And Jack believed him. The majestic grey horse beneath him didn't move a muscle until Joel asked if he was ready.

Joel acknowledged his nod in response, and said, "Come along Eliza." And on hearing his instruction, she quietly positioned herself behind Penelope, and plodded along at a steady pace.

Penelope and Joel led them along the track towards the furthest field of Pine Trees.

"Our winter paddock," offered Joel, as they ambled through the long grass and pretty meadow flowers. They headed down the small sloping bank and across the gently flowing rocky river, all the while Eliza's surefooted hooves never missed a step. A narrow track met them on the opposite side of the river, and the horses slowly climbed the steep slope, taking them deep into the forest. Jack could smell the musty smell of the pines, and sweet scent of the horses sweat. In the clear, fresh air, Jack felt a calmness envelope him. He was beginning to think that Phoebe was right. *When is she not?* Her world of horses was becoming more and more appealing to him the more time he spent with them. Pine Trees, with the peaceful flowing river marking its boundaries, the mysterious forest, and the horses, was truly remarkable, and he could now understand why Phoebe wholeheartedly believed that this intoxicating, enchanting place was her paradise home.

"She's not in a good way," Joel finally volunteered, bringing Jack back down to reality with a bump. "It's not just the injuries she's suffered, it's the psychological impact as well."

Having limited knowledge of what actually happened to Phoebe, he was secretly hoping that Joel would divulge the true account of what she had been through. Bridget's message had purely been perfunctory. All he knew was that she'd been in a car accident and would be in hospital for weeks, and wasn't up to seeing visitors just yet. He knew nothing of real substance and nothing to ease his rapidly rising fear of whether she would survive what had happened to her.

"I know Mum's been keeping you in the loop," he continued. "Phoebe spoke very highly of you, we both presumed you were becoming a permanent fixture in her life?"

Jack was pleased to be able to clarify both his feelings and his budding relationship with Phoebe. "Yes, very much so. Phoebe means the world to me. She was supposed to meet my daughter Chloe on the day of the fete. Chloe is very much looking forward to getting to know her, and to welcoming her into our family. Although, I must admit Joel, your Mum hasn't been all that specific about what has happened to her."

Joel seemed content with his honest and open reply, and finally, it seemed that Joel trusted him to tell him the full magnitude of her accident.

"The intense impact of the vehicles caused an explosion. Phoebe was trapped in her car with no escape from the flames." Joel turned to look at him, and his eyes penetrated Jack's. "She's been severely burned, all down the left side of her body."

Jack felt nausea rising within him. The fear she must have felt, the claustrophobia, the burning. *Oh holy jesus, no wonder Bridget didn't tell me.*

"As well as the physical injuries, we don't know, nor do the doctors know, how long it will take her to come to terms with what she has suffered," Joel said gravely.

"I hope she knows that I'm here for her, whenever she needs me," Jack said. "Joel, will you tell her that for me please? I know she's not up for seeing me yet, but I'm waiting. I'll be there as soon as she needs me. And anything in the meantime that I can do for her, or you and Bridget, please let me. Let me help in any way that I can, even if it's to feed the horses so you and Bridget don't have to leave her."

"Thank you," replied Joel. "Mum and I really appreciate the ffer."

The two men became lost in their own thoughts, and silence descended upon them again. The soft hoofbeats beneath them and the light breeze whistling through the trees were the only sounds to reach their ears as the two men, and the horses, steadily made their way home.

Bridget

Bridget lowered herself down onto William's deep straw bed, placed her head in her hands and wept. Her beautiful, darling girl. How could such a terrible thing happen to her? *Why Phoebe? Why my daughter, who has been through so much already losing her father? Why did the driver, who had been the cause of the accident, walk away with only cuts and bruises? Why could life be so incredibly cruel?* Round and round went her thoughts, so many questions that she would never receive an answer for. Great big, ugly sobs poured out of her. Finally, alone, in the privacy of William's stable, she could let it all out, all the pent-up frustration and anger that she could not reveal in front of anyone. She had to be strong for Phoebe, and for Joel. She refused to let them see her like this, refused to allow them to think that she could not look after her family.

She felt William's soft nose nuzzle her fingers. Inelegantly wiping her nose and eyes with the back of her shirt sleeve, she sniffed an unladylike sniff, then opened her arms to envelop her miniature best friend in a comforting hug. Burying her face in his mane, she breathed in his familiar horsey scent.

"My dear little William," she whispered into his ear, "what ever would I do without you?" And she heard his deep, tender nicker in reply. He rested his head on her shoulder as she held him tightly and continued to weep into his mane. Her little friend didn't move. She had no idea how long they stayed embraced. Time seemed to stand still whilst she poured her heart out into his silken mane, her loyal best friend, by her side, just like he always was. Once her breathing steadied, and her tears dried, she slowly pulled away from him. Holding his dear little face in both her hands, she planted an affectionate kiss on his nose. "How about some peppermints?" she asked him. And rummaging around in her coat pocket, she retrieved a packet of polo mints, William's favourite. Gently taking the proffered polo mints, one at a time from her hand, Bridget listened to the satisfying crunch as William greedily gobbled up his treats.

Treats devoured, Bridget gave William one last affectionate pet, and then turned him out into the paddock with Eliza and Penelope. Her self-imposed therapy time with William was over. It was time to freshen up, make herself presentable, then go to the hospital to support her daughter.

Bridget momentarily paused outside Phoebe's hospital room door. She slapped on her biggest smile, and what she hoped was a cheery voice, before bursting in and saying, "Phoebe, sweetheart, how are you feeling today?"

Phoebe was sitting up in bed, munching on the grapes she had given her yesterday.

"Mum, hi," she replied, with a forced smile. "The doctor has just gone. Apparently, the burns are healing well, and the bandages should be coming off next week."

"Well, that's great news," replied Bridget, before noticing Phoebe's scowl, then continued, "Isn't it?"

"Once the bandages come off there will be no hiding from the scars then," Phoebe said, and Bridget could see the anxiety clearly in her eyes and stiffened posture. "I'll have to wear gloves, shirts buttoned up to the neck and long skirts and dresses for the rest of my life. I'll probably scare the life out of children!" she snarked.

"Oh, love, don't be silly," replied Bridget, stepping towards her daughter, and wrapping her arms tightly around her. "No one will ever judge you for having scars. Everyone loves you for who you are, Phoebe. Outward scars do not change who you are, and I promise you sweetheart, you are still you. And like the doctor told us right at the beginning, the severe brightness of the scars will dull over time."

Bridget let Phoebe relax into her arms, and as she softly stroked her hair, she felt her shoulder dampen with Phoebe's silent tears. Her heart ached for her quirky, clever, wonderful daughter. And her heart broke at the fact that she could not turn back the clock, she could not undo what had happened. Her daughter would forever have to live with the consequences of someone else's thoughtless, selfish actions. She would forever be haunted by the memory of being trapped in a burning car, and have to live with her beautiful body covered in scars.

Drying her eyes with the sleeve of her dressing gown, Phoebe pulled away from her mother, and gestured for her mother to lie side by side with her on the narrow hospital bed. Bridget climbed up and snuggled up next to Phoebe. Bridget saw a little smile twitch in the corner of Phoebe's mouth.

"What is it?" she asked, curious to find out what had lightened Phoebe's spirits.

"Mr Parker," giggled Phoebe. "He's a nice man. Is there anything you'd like to tell me about him?" she asked with playful, quizzical eyes.

Bridget felt herself blush at the unexpected turn in the conversation.

"You're blushing!" exclaimed Phoebe. "I knew it, you like him, don't you?"

They were both giggling like a pair of teenagers, and Bridget confessed that she did indeed like Mr Charles Parker.

"I'm so pleased for you, Mum. You deserve someone nice. You've been on your own too long. Joel likes him too. He owes me five quid!"

"What!" laughed Bridget. "What have you two been betting on now?"

"That I could get you to tell that Mr Parker was your boyfriend before he could!" Phoebe laughed in reply.

Bridget felt a little sparkle of the old Phoebe, which led her to ask the question, and what of you and Jack? He seems like a lovely man."

Phoebe's face darkened on hearing Jack's name. "Oh, I don't think that will come to anything," she replied.

"But I thought you were really fond of him, and looking forward to meeting Chloe? Have you thanked him for the flowers he sent you?" pushed Bridget.

"That was before I looked like this," said Phoebe. "How could anyone possibly want me now? And no, I haven't contacted him at all yet. I just don't know what to say to him," she admitted.

Bridget's heart went out to her. *How could she possibly think that nobody would want her?* Bridget couldn't believe it.

"Sweetheart, look at me," she said. Phoebe's tear-stained eyes met hers. "You are beautiful, Phoebe, just as you are. Is this why you won't let Jack visit you? You're worried that he won't want to be with you once he sees the extent of your injuries?"

Bridget watched the tears roll down Phoebe's face as she nodded. "The worst thing is," Phoebe stuttered between her tears, "he'll probably feel that he has to stay with me, because of what I look like. That he was doing the 'gentlemanly thing' or something. I don't want to be anyone's pity girlfriend, Mum. It's better if I stop it now so he doesn't feel guilted into being with me. It's for the best."

"Do you not think that Jack should be able to make that decision for himself, love? What if he's like me and Joel, and can see past the scars and loves you for who you really are? And quite frankly, you still have the prettiest face of all the girls in Cornwall," Bridget said, smiling at her daughter as she gently moved a lock of Phoebe's golden hair out of her face, and tucked it behind her ear.

Phoebe smiled in reply. "You have to say that, you're my Mum!"

A loud knock at the door made them both jump.

"Who is it? called out Bridget, sliding off the bed to straighten her clothes and look presentable for this mysterious visitor, whoever they might be.

"It's nurse Debbie," replied the voice, and Bridget instantly recognised her as soon as she stepped into the room. "I have someone here who would like to meet you Phoebe, if you're feeling up to it?"

Bridget looked at her daughter, who had a curious and slightly bewildered look on her face. Before either of them had a chance to reply, a bubbly red-headed girl bounced into the room.

"Phoebe, it is so good to finally meet you. I have been so looking forward to seeing you. I'm Mel." Mel bounded over to Phoebe and handed over the huge box of chocolates that she was carrying.

Phoebe's raised eyebrows and quizzical look prompted Mel to elaborate on her own introduction. I'm the one that found you," she beamed.

Bridget and Phoebe eyed up the petite, young woman standing before them. "But we were told that the person who found me was the one who pulled me out of the car?"

"Yep, that was me," grinned Mel, flexing her slender arms in jest. "See, I'm stronger than I look!"

"But, you're tiny!" blurted out Phoebe.

Giggling away, Mel continued, "Luckily I always have my penknife on me, you know, for cutting baler twine, so I was able to cut you out of your jammed seat belt and drag you out," she said, smiling at them both.

Bridget and Phoebe just stared at the little woman who was their hero.

Mel ploughed on, unperturbed by their silence. "Percy and I - Percy's my horse - we've just moved in with my boyfriend," she gushed. "His family own the farm just along the lane where I found you."

"Phoebe has a horse, don't you love," Bridget chipped in, warming to this easy-going, kind-natured girl.

"Yes, her name's Penelope. My yard is only a ten-minute hack from your boyfriend's farm," replied Phoebe.

"You do? How wonderful, Percy and I have been desperate to find someone local to ride with. How amazing is this. When you're up and about do you think we could ride together?" Mel asked eagerly.

Bridget offered Mel the chair closest to Phoebe's bed. "Why don't I go and get us all a cup of tea? We can enjoy them with some of those chocolates you brought, Mel."

"Oh yes please," replied Mel, settling herself on the chair. "I just knew we were going to be friends! Now tell me everything about Penelope. Have you got a picture of her? Here, this is my Percy," she said, taking her phone out of her pocket to show off her beloved horse.

Bridget slipped out of the room. *What a whirlwind that girl is!* she thought. *And exactly what Phoebe needs right now.* It had not gone unnoticed by Bridget that not once had Mel looked at Phoebe's bandaged body, and not once had she mentioned or shown any curiosity at what might be beneath them. They had no impact on how keen she was to meet Phoebe and had no impact on their shared love of horses. *Hopefully this friendly, kind stranger will give Phoebe the confidence boost she is very much in need of.* Feeling the lightest she had felt since Phoebe's accident, Bridget skipped off to get herself and the girls some tea.

Lilly

Lilly sat down at her kitchen table and sighed. Oliver and Isla were tucked up in bed, fast asleep, and Milo was snoozing at her feet. It had been two weeks since Phoebe's terrible accident, and ever since she learned what had happened, she felt unsettled. A restlessness had taken over her. She couldn't focus properly at work, something she just couldn't understand because she adored her job. She lacked motivation to engage or play with Oliver, which then left her consumed with guilt. And as much as she hated to admit it, she was grateful to have hardly seen Joel since the accident. Between his work schedule and visiting Phoebe at the hospital, it hadn't left much time for dating. She understood, of course she did, and he had been so kind and apologetic that she felt buried under a landslide of even more guilt, because she in fact did not want to see him at all, and his staying away from her was a relief.

She got up and made a cup of tea, the restlessness taunting her, leaving her unable to concentrate or focus on any one thing for any length of time. Steaming mug of tea in her hand, she padded into her sitting room, and settled herself on the sofa. Milo jumped up beside her and rested his head in her lap.

"I can't carry on like this, can I?" she said to her dog. And Milo blinked a long slow blink back at her. And then Isla sauntered into the sitting room, jumped up on the arm of the sofa, and looked directly at Lilly. *How unusual,* thought Lilly, taken by surprise. Isla never strayed from Oliver during the night. Only when Oliver woke, did they come downstairs for breakfast together. For her to leave him during the night was most out of character.

"Are you ok, Isla?" Lilly asked, tickling her under her chin until she purred. *She looks fine,* thought Lilly, running her hands over Islas body checking for any scratches or sores that she might have missed. *Nope, healthy as ever,* she confirmed.

Flummoxed as to why she had been graced with Isla's presence, but grateful to be in the company of both of her furry friends, she stroked the snoring Milo with one hand and the purring Isla with the other. After a few minutes of quiet, comfortable silence between the three of them, Isla slowly pulled away from Lilly's touch, glided across the back of the sofa, and with an effortless jump, landed on the dresser. She looked placidly at Lilly, whilst sitting carefully between the precious photographs Lilly had on display. She curled her tail around the photograph of Lilly and Annie, and Lilly felt the back of her throat burn, and hot tears trickling down her cheek. Staring back at her cat, she nodded.

The sound of her mobile phone bleeping with a message startled her. Drying her eyes, she retrieved her phone and saw Minnie's name on the screen.

Hi Lilly, So sorry it's such short notice. Oliver free tomorrow? I've been given two tickets for go carting – Damian would love it if Oliver could join him? He can stay for dinner and sleep over too as it's Saturday night? Minnie x

Lilly liked Minnie. Her little boy Damian was lovely, and he and Oliver had become firm friends. Minnie was a single parent too, and they often helped each other out if ever needed. Minnie was also an avid tea drinker like herself, and they both enjoyed sitting in each other's kitchens, supping large mugs of tea, catching up on all the latest school gossip whenever time permitted, whilst the boys happily played together.

She looked up at Isla, still positioned amongst the photographs, with her tail circling the picture of Lilly and Annie. Lilly felt the strangest feeling engulf her, it was almost as if the little mystical cat sitting before her had concocted a play date for Oliver, allowing her the option to have some time for herself. To do something that had been at the back of her mind since Phoebe's accident, but she had kept it buried in there, too afraid to open Pandora's box. Isla blinked at her, *Am I ready now?* she asked herself.

She quickly typed a reply to Minnie.

Wow, yes please. Oliver would love too. Thank you. Lilly x

Ping, message sent. She did not have Oliver to use as an excuse now. It was time to go home.

Lilly squeezed the excited little bundle that was her nephew. "Now, you be a good boy for Minnie," she told him, kissing the top of his head before releasing him.

"I will, Aunt Lilly," he replied, before scampering off to play with Damian and Milo in the garden.

Lilly turned to her friend. "Thanks so much for having him, Min, and you're sure you're ok with feeding Isla this evening and tomorrow morning?" she questioned.

"Of course! No problem at all. You and Milo enjoy your night away. Oliver will be fine, I promise you," replied Minnie, reaching out and giving her a hug. "Now off you go, enjoy your alone time!"

Laughing along with her friend, Lilly replied, "I promise to repay the favour soon!"

"Boys," called out Minnie, scooping up Oliver's overnight bag on her way out. "It's time to go. Who wants ice cream before we go go-carting?"

Lilly could hear the shrieks of excitement as Minnie bundled two very excited boys into her car. A brief wave from the happy little party, and they were gone.

Lilly glanced around her quiet, empty home, slipped her handbag over her arm, picked up her little overnight case and Milo's bag of bits and bobs needed for their trip away, and with a quick glance in her hallway mirror, she gave herself a determined nod. It was time.

"Come along Milo," she called, opening the car door for him to jump up onto the front seat beside her. "We're going to Dorset."

Memory after memory washed over Lilly as her car trundled along the familiar Dorset roads. Dorset had been her home for so many years, and she had been happy there. They all had been so happy. She pulled up outside her old house. Her little semi-detached rented cottage, with the peacock blue wooden gate and blooming rose bushes lining the right-hand side of the garden next to the little gravel path, and the open space of neatly trimmed lawn to the left. It all looked exactly like she had left it all those months ago. Oliver had walked for the first time in that garden. She closed her eyes and remembered the thirteen-month-old Oliver, toddling on the soft grass. She had been so excited to video him with her phone and send his first steps, captured forever, to her sister, so they could share the moment together.

She watched the new occupier unlatch the gate, heard the crunching of their footsteps across the gravel, then saw them slip inside the house. It was their home now. For Lilly, it was part of her previous life.

Starting the ignition, she turned to Milo. "Time for memory lane part two." And she directed her car out of the quiet little cul-de-sac and travelled the ten-minute journey to Annie's house. A beautiful, imposing, detached, red brick, four-bedroom house. *The perfect family home,* she thought, and it had been. She could picture Annie's garden, the most picturesque of English gardens. Her elegant outdoor table laden with food and the smell of sausages sizzling on the barbecue. Annie pushing Oliver on the swing, and Lilly collecting flowers from the huge, well-stocked garden, to make their lunch table look pretty. They had spent so many family gatherings together at her home, celebrating birthdays, anniversaries, festive holidays, not to mention the many evenings she and Annie had curled up on the sofa together, glass of wine in their hands, enjoying each other's company and chatting late into the night. Truth be told, it had always felt like Lilly's second home. She could come and go as she pleased, the door was always open for her, and her wonderful, darling sister welcomed her with open arms, each and every time she arrived on her doorstep.

Escaping to her private world of how things used to be, Lilly lost all sense of time. Her mind grappled to recall all the little, intricate details, so she could hold on to the perfect memories forever. She so desperately wished that she could just step out of her car, stroll up the driveway, knock on the door, and be enveloped into her sister's warm embrace, just one last time. The tears streamed down her face knowing that she would never feel her sister's arms around her again, nor be greeted with her warm smile.

She felt Milo nudge her knee and whine, bringing her back into the present. "Oh Milo," she gushed, checking her watch, "you've been cooped up in the car for hours!" Giving him a quick stroke, she pushed her heartache aside, started up the car, and said, "Cross your legs for five more minutes! I'm going to take you to mine and Oliver's favourite place."

Stepping out of the car in the beach car park, Lilly inhaled the fresh sea breeze deeply. She and Oliver used to visit this coastline often. The long stretch of golden sand allowed plenty of open space for Oliver to run and play and fill his lungs with healthy sea air. They would roll up their trousers and paddle in the lapping waves, and as the cold water danced around their toes, Oliver would shriek with delight. She pictured his dancing eyes and gleeful smile; it was one of her most cherished memories.

Now it was early evening, and the beach was almost deserted. She led Milo down the sand dunes path, then unclipped his lead. "Off you go," she said to him, "go play!" And she watched him bound away, galloping across the sand, exuberant at finally being allowed to stretch his legs.

Lilly slipped off her shoes and socks, rolled up her jeans, and walked across the wet sand. She felt a rush of adrenaline each time an icy cold wave rolled over her bare feet. With the gentle sea breeze flitting around her hair, she walked, and she cried. Deep, heavy, throaty sobs poured out of her. All the suppressed feelings from the last two weeks could be contained no more. The fear and anxiety she felt on hearing that Phoebe had been in a car accident had brought back all of the harrowing memories of the day she received the tragic news about Annie to the forefront of her mind. And the feelings of shame when jealousy erupted through her whole being when she found out that Phoebe would live.

She couldn't comprehend why she would think such terrible things. She would never wish any harm to come of Phoebe. But the nonsensical thoughts kept penetrating her mind. Why did Phoebe get to live when her own sister died? Why did Oliver have to lose his mother, and Joel got to keep his sister? All of these terrible, horrible thoughts that she could not rid herself of. She didn't want to think them. And that was the reason she couldn't be around Joel. The utter humiliation she felt, and the fear that he could somehow read her thoughts. And her merry-go-round mind did not stop there. She felt swallowed up by terror that she could lose Joel. The more she let him into her life, the more she fell in love with him. What if something happened to him? What if she lost him? She didn't think her broken heart could cope with another colossal loss. Life could be so very, very hard.

Lilly strode along the beach, finally allowing her mind to process all of her shocking and appalling thoughts. And she allowed her overbearing grief to flow. The tears streamed, her body ached, her mind whirled, and on she trudged.

It was pitch black by the time she returned to her car. The sky was clear, and the bright moon cast a sparkling glow upon the ocean. Milo, exhausted from his long walk, eagerly climbed in beside her, and together, they made their way to the hotel. Collapsing on the hotel bed, with Milo curled up beside her, Lilly fell into a deep sleep.

She woke the next morning, and the heavy, grey cloud that had suffocated her for the past few weeks was now gone. She reached out to find her faithful friend, still by her side, like he always was. She scratched his ears and told him, "One more place to visit."

"Hi Annie," said Lilly softly, placing a bunch of hand-picked, hedge row flowers on her grave. "I've missed you." Lilly and Milo settled themselves on the grass beside her grave, and Lilly continued, "Oliver is doing so well at school. He has a cat, Isla, but I think you already knew that didn't you? And this is Milo," she said, reaching out to caress his ears. "Our dog. My best friend." And once she started to talk, it all came tumbling out. Joel, Phoebe's accident, her fears, her hopes, and her life in Cornwall.

Mentioning Cornwall and telling her sister how wonderful hers and Oliver's lives were, and how they had settled so effortlessly into village life, made her realise that Cornwall was where she wanted to be. The past was in the past, and her home and future were in Cornwall. Her appreciation for what she had, right now, started to bubble away inside her. She bade her farewells to her sister and affectionately kissed her head stone, before walking away, with Milo trotting along by her side. Returning to Dorset had been necessary, but Lilly felt she was now able to close the door on her past in order to make room for her future. It was time to go home to Cornwall.

Phoebe

"All ready?" asked Bridget, clutching Phoebe's hospital bag in one hand, and offering her other for Phoebe to take hold of.

Taking her mother's arm, Phoebe gave a tentative smile. "Yep, everything is packed, let's go home."

Sitting in the front seat of Bridget's car, Phoebe asked, "Could we pop in and see Pen on the way home please? It's been almost four weeks, I'm desperate to see her."

Phoebe saw Bridget's lips twitch into a smile, "I thought you would say that! Yes, of course. But straight home afterwards, the doctor said you need plenty of rest."

Phoebe felt her pulse quicken when they pulled into Pine Trees driveway. It had been agony staying away from her horse for so long, to be away from her beloved Pine Trees for almost a month. She clicked her door open before Bridget even finished parking the car, and then eagerly covered the ground between her and the paddock gate way. Sliding open the latch, she called her horse, and stepped inside. Penelope jerked her head up from grazing, her body poised and alert on hearing Phoebe's voice. Phoebe called her name again. Penelope exploded into canter from stand still, and Phoebe's emotions swelled within her as she watched her elegant horse stride across the meadow to greet her.

"Oh Penelope," she gushed, wrapping her arms around her friend and burying her head into her mane. Penelope rested her head on Phoebe's shoulder, and they stood together, inhaling each other's familiar, comforting scent, so very grateful to be in one another's company again.

"I've missed you so much," cried Phoebe, and Penelope nickered her, deep, intimate nicker in reply, her own expression for sharing her feelings of being parted from her friend for such a long time. It was the nicker she used just for Phoebe, for the secrets they shared amidst each other's whispers. Phoebe ran her hands along Penelope's smooth fur, feeling the strength of her muscles, the curves of her body, and she scratched her favourite spots. Her horse relaxed under her touch, her eyes closed, her back leg cocked, as she openly relished the attention her mistress bestowed on her. When Phoebe moved to her head, and lightly stroked her face with her fingertips, Penelope opened her eyes, and nuzzled her deeply scarred hand.

"You know, don't you girl," whispered Phoebe. And Penelope continued to snuffle her wrist, her arm, her shoulder, and her neck. She rested her soft nose in the crook of Phoebe's neck, gently warming her with her sweet breath. Phoebe closed her eyes and remembered their morning ride, the last ride before the accident. She felt a sense of irony that she and Penelope had shared the most perfect, magical ride, before the most terrible, tragic accident occurred. *The balance of the universe,* she thought, *with perfection comes devastation, and that is most certainly what I was handed on that fateful day.*

She looked deep into Penelope's soft, kind eyes. "The accident still doesn't take away the wonderful ride we shared in our enchanting forest, and all the rides we will share together in the future. I can't wait!" she told her horse. She felt genuinely excited about having something positive to think about and focus on. Being back at Pine Trees, with her darling Penelope, reminded her that all was not lost. Her paradise home was still paradise, and better yet, off the beaten track so she wouldn't be bumping into anyone and dealing with their shocked reaction at the sight of her. Here, tucked away, in the privacy of her private land, she could be alone, with her horses, just as she liked to be. And that, at least, was something to feel positive about.

Phoebe heard her mother call out, breaking the spell between them. "Come along now Phoebe. Say goodbye to Pen, you need to rest."

Planting a kiss on Penelope's nose, she said, "I'll see you tomorrow, girl."

Phoebe watched Penelope glide across the paddock to where Eliza and William were snoozing, and after casting her mistress one last glance, she turned her attention back to grazing with her herd.

Bridget ushered Phoebe into the sitting room as soon as they arrived home, and to her surprise, the coffee table was covered with presents and flowers.

"All for you," announced Bridget.

Phoebe looked at the pile of gifts in awe.

"Settle down," said Bridget, patting the sofa and fussing over her. "I'll go and make us a cup of tea."

"Mum, I'm fine!" laughed Phoebe, but secretly she was enjoying her mother being so attentive. Sitting side by side, sipping their tea and munching on homemade cinnamon buns, Bridget gestured to the pile of presents. "Do you want to open them now? Or are you tired?"

"Presents!" announced Phoebe. She'd never had much patience waiting for any kind of present, and there was no way she would be able to rest properly knowing there were presents waiting to be opened! One by one, her mother handed the beautifully wrapped gifts to her.

A beautiful cream rose plant was gifted from the ladies at Hollybrook Stables, to be planted when she finally moved to Pine Trees, and a basket of home-made brownies. *Mmmmmm delicious,* thought Phoebe, helping herself to one, before moving on to the next parcel.

It was elegantly wrapped in lavender tissue paper. Phoebe unfolded the most exquisite, satin, navy blue shirt.

"Oh, how gorgeous, who's it from?" asked Bridget.

Dear Phoebe, I'm so sorry to hear about your accident. Jack told me you liked blue, and I hope this material feels soft and comforting against your skin. If it causes you any irritation at all, please let me know and I will exchange it for something else. We all miss you at the office. Laura x

After reading the card out loud, Phoebe was speechless. "But," she stammered. "I thought she didn't like me. What a lovely, thoughtful gift."

Her mother met her eyes and smiled. "People show their true colours during times like these Phoebe. I think there might be more to this Laura than meets the eye, don't you?"

"Yes Mum, I think you're right."

"Ok, next present," said Bridget, handing over a large package.

"Ooooooh it's from Ellen!" Ripping open the paper, she found a bright blue saddle pad. Diamanté stones trimmed the edge, with Penelope's name delicately embroidered in white stitching on one side, and her own on the other. "Oh Mum! Isn't it amazing!" And she slipped out the card to read.

Phoebes, I know the done thing is to get someone flowers and chocolates, but let's face it, horsey stuff is what you really want! I saw another rider at a show last week with this design and thought of you. I just had to order one for you! Jupiter and I can't wait to go riding with you. Lots of love, Ellen xxx

"She knows me so well! I can't wait to try it out, how very kind of her," exclaimed Phoebe, as gratitude swept through her with how many wonderful friends she had.

A homemade card from Lilly and Oliver accompanied a large box of chocolates, and then a final card was left sitting on the table. Bridget handed it to her. A vibrant flash of colour fell out of the envelope. Butterflies in every colour were splashed over the card and it brought a smile to Phoebe's face.

"Oh, what an exquisite card," said Phoebe.

Dear Phoebe, I'm so sorry that we didn't get to meet at the fete. I was really looking forward to it. I hope you feel better soon. Love Chloe x

Phoebe passed the card over to her mother without uttering a word, for her to read it herself.

"She's a lovely girl Phoebe, you would really like her," her mother said quietly.

"I can't think about that now, Mum. I need more time, but it was very sweet of her to send me such a beautiful card."

"Yes, it was," replied Bridget, but not pushing the matter further. "Ok, last one, then off to bed for a rest." Then she handed over a large, brown papered parcel, tied up with string.

Phoebe's world slowed when the final gift revealed itself from behind the plain brown paper.

"Where did you get this from?" gasped Phoebe.

"Oh, that must have been what Joel collected from town the other day, I must have added it to your present pile by mistake. What is it?" enquired her mother.

Phoebe slowly turned the intricately designed oak frame, proudly showing off the picture she had taken of Jack and Pixie all those weeks ago. "This present isn't for me," admitted Phoebe. "It's from me. I was on my way to collect this when I had my accident. It was a gift for Jack."

Phoebe stared into the picture and felt Jack's sparkling green eyes stare right back at her. An unbearable sadness washed over her on seeing him again. She had spent so long trying to rid herself of all thoughts of him, desperate to try and forget the feelings she had for him. She told herself time and time again that nothing had actually happened, nothing between them had been confirmed. It was best to break away now, from whatever it was that had been between them, to save them both the heartache of what would inevitably come once he saw how terribly disfigured her skin had become. She tried to convince herself that she was doing the right thing staying away from him, for Jack as much as herself.

If you truly loved someone, the kindest thing to do was to let them go, and that is what she felt she was doing for Jack. She would not make him feel beholden to her just because of what had happened. If he simply stayed with her because he felt sorry for her, she knew that would be a recipe for disaster for both of them.

But seeing him now, his handsome, kind, caring face, brought all of her buried, pent-up emotions right up to the surface. Her shoulders heaved, and her throat ached from trying to hold back her tears. Her mother's arm slowly snaked around the back of her shoulders, and on feeling her comforting touch, the floodgates finally opened, and her tears spilled.

"Oh, sweetheart," cried her mother, pulling her towards her and holding her tightly.

With her mother stroking her hair, and smoothing her back, she sobbed about what could have been. She wept for what her life once was, and she cried, deep, heavy tears, for Jack.

When her heartache finally ebbed, and her tears slowed, her mother said, "Phoebe, darling, I know it's none of my business but I'm going to say it anyway. I can't bear to see you like this. Especially as you haven't allowed Jack to share his side of the story with you. I understand your hesitation for seeing him, honestly, I do, but don't you think it is worth at least knowing for sure that this is what Jack wants. He must be as equally heartbroken as you for not being able to see you. You haven't contacted him in four weeks, Phoebe. Imagine how he must be feeling? Imagine if it was the other way around?"

Guilt swelled in Phoebe on hearing her mother's words, adding to the swirl of emotions she was already experiencing. She finally understood the truth of what she had inadvertently done to Jack. And she didn't like it. She didn't like to acknowledge how selfish she had been, how unkind her actions had been, and all just to protect herself. Not once had she thought how her silence would affect Jack, and she felt ashamed. *The old Phoebe would never have done such a thing,* she thought, chastising herself.

"And from what I have learned about Jack, from the little I know of him," Bridget continued, "I doubt your scars will make a blind bit of difference to him, Phoebe. I think you should give the man some credit for liking you, simply for you. If you want to end things with him, then that is your decision, and I will support you one hundred percent. But not like this. You owe it to him to be honest and tell him to his face that whatever it was that has been between you is now over. Or," her mother said, taking a deep breath, "or, you could trust him. Trust that he is the decent, compassionate man you know him to be and allow him to love you for you, just the way you are."

"But what if he doesn't," whispered Phoebe.

"Then he doesn't," replied her mother, in a very matter of fact tone. "Your world will not end Phoebe, and your brother and I, and Penelope, will support you through it, just like we always have. But until you see him, you will never know. And I for one would rather go through life thinking at least I tried, rather than regretting what I didn't try."

Sitting up and wiping her tears, she nodded. "You're right, Mum. I've behaved appallingly towards him. I'll contact him soon," she said, with a determined edge in her voice. "Thank you, Mum, I needed to hear that."

Leaning in for a quick, affectionate hug, Bridget said, "Now then, how about we sample some of these chocolates that Lilly sent you!"

"Definitely!" replied Phoebe, feeling much happier than she had in a long time after sharing her feelings so openly with her mum. Tomorrow is always a new day.

Joel

Joel reached out and tickled Kit's velvety nose, pondering whether he had, in fact, gone completely bonkers, or if he had done the most wonderful thing ever. *Time will tell,* he mused.

Last week, Joel had arrived at a local livery yard to shoe Kit, just like he had been doing every eight weeks for the last three years. His owner, Mrs Jenkins, he liked very much. Kit was always immaculate, ready and waiting for his arrival and never failed to behave like a perfect gentleman. A happy chap is how Joel would describe him, and most definitely treated like Mrs Jenkins' second child. The pony wanted for nothing. Unfortunately, Mrs Jenkins confessed that due to her daughter's progression, the time had come to find Kit a new home. Although she utterly adored him, she could not afford the livery and day-to-day costs for two horses, and her daughter's new horse would be arriving in three days. She wanted to do what was right by Kit; he would not be sold on to just anyone. He deserved a loving home, like what he had become accustomed too. She asked whether Joel knew of anyone looking for a pony? Anyone coming with Joel's recommendation would definitely give a potential owner a foot in the door.

Joel had taken a step back and looked at Kit, really looked at him. Ten years old, fourteen hands, skewbald cob, with a very handsome face and a gentle, easy-going temperament. He'd been to competitions, fun rides, pony club camp and marched along happily when hacking out on his own. Personally, Joel thought it was a huge mistake to replace him, but it wasn't his place to say.

Instead, from nowhere, he heard himself saying, "Actually Mrs Jenkins, I do know someone. Me!"

"Well," he said to the little horse as he watched Lilly's car pull into his drive way, "we're about to find out."

"Hi Joel," Lilly said shyly, stepping onto the yard.

Joel felt the usual flutter in his heart at seeing her. They had barely spent any time together over the last five weeks, and he realised how neglectful he had been, taking advantage of her kind and generous nature, just expecting her to be available for him when he had the time. He had not been fair. And he hoped that he would be able to make it up her, to show her how much she meant to him, and how he longed for them to pick up where they left off before Phoebe's accident.

"Who's this?" she enquired, tentatively stroking Kit, as Milo and Katie greeted each other ecstatically before bouncing off to play in the paddocks.

"His name's Kit. Lovely little chap, isn't he?" replied Joel.

Lilly giggled as Kit's whiskers tickled her fingers. "Yes, yes he is," she agreed.

"I thought you might like to ride him today instead of Eliza?" Joel asked. He had used riding as an excuse to entice Lilly over to Pine Trees. Once Phoebe left the hospital and he knew that his mum would be taking care of her at home, his protectiveness for his sister relaxed, and it wasn't until he had his epiphany at the livery yard with Mrs Jenkins and Kit, that it dawned on him how selfishly he had behaved towards Lilly.

He wanted to make amends - he needed to make amends - and he hoped the little horse would help him. Suggesting a riding lesson gave them something to focus on, rather than the elephant in the room of him basically dropping her like a stone. He didn't mean for it to have happened, truth be told, but he had been so swept up with Phoebe and work that the days rolled into one, and the weeks just slipped by. He'd sent her daily messages, of course, but that was not the same as being with her, showing her that she was just as important to him as Phoebe. And she agreed to come to Pine Trees to ride, so that at least, was a step in the right direction for him.

"I'll saddle him up then?" suggested Joel.

"Is he safe?" she asked. "As safe as Eliza?"

"One hundred percent. Kit is the perfect gentleman in every way," he assured her, and was rewarded with her shy smile again.

"Don't leave me," Lilly said, with a hint of fear in her voice when the three of them were standing in the makeshift paddock schooling area.

"Not for a moment," Joel replied, smiling up at her. "This is a lunge line, it's much longer than a lead rope so it will give you a bit more freedom, but I'll still have complete control, ok?"

"Ok," she replied, and nodded.

Joel watched Lilly's confidence slowly build as the steady, reliable Kit walked carefully in circles around Joel. Her stature changed from clinging tightly on to his mane, to holding his reins in a much more relaxed position.

"You ok up there?" asked Joel.

"Yes! He's so lovely, Joel," gushed Lilly, leaning forward to stroke his neck.

"Ready to have a go on your own?" he asked. He noticed her hesitation before adding, "I'll walk next to you, right by your side."

"Ok then," she agreed.

It wasn't long before Joel was able to resume his position, standing in the middle of the paddock, and he was watching Lilly ride Kit, alone.

"I'm doing it!" squealed Lilly. "I'm riding a horse!"

"Yes, you are!" Joel replied, his voice full of pride. "You and Kit have been working for an hour, shall we give him a rest now?"

"Really? Blimey, that time has flown by! Yes, of course, Kit needs his rest."

Brushing down Kit on the yard together, Joel felt it was time to broach the subject of his neglect. His time with Lilly felt just like it always did. Relaxed, enjoyable, effortless, and he wanted to be honest with her.

"I'm so sorry for shutting you out, Lilly. For not giving you my time when Phoebe was in hospital. It wasn't fair on you," he explained.

Lilly continued to brush Kit. Slowly but surely, she rhythmically made her way all over his body, ensuring each and every last hair was soothed to perfection. After a brief pause, which felt like an eternity to Joel, even though he knew he must wait for Lilly to find her own words in response, she spoke.

"To be honest, Joel, I needed time away from you."

He felt a little taken aback by her reply. It was not what he had been expecting at all.

"I actually went away, to Dorset," she confided, "to see Annie."

The magnitude of what Lilly must have been through over the last five weeks suddenly dawned on Joel. How could he have been so stupid to forget about Annie, and how she died. He had been so wrapped up in himself, that the thought never crossed his mind. And to make it worse, even though Phoebe had been in a terrible way, he and Bridget were told right from the start that she would survive. And Annie had not. Lilly had received the same phone call he had from a hospital in Dorset, but the conversation she'd had to endure had taken a very different turn.

Her sister had been killed on impact. Her sister had died and left behind a little boy that Lilly was raising on her own. Guilt flowed through him as he recognised his own appalling behaviour. He had always prided himself on supporting his mother and sister, through anything and everything. Whenever they needed him, he was there. Neglecting to support Lilly, the woman he loved, during such a traumatic time, was a colossal failure on his part.

"Lilly, I'm so very sorry I wasn't there for you."

"Don't be," Lilly replied. "I didn't want you to be. I needed to get through it on my own. I didn't realise how important it was to revisit the past until I was there. I wanted to say I'm sorry to you. For being so wrapped up in myself that I didn't support you properly with Phoebe. I'm truly sorry, Joel."

Joel couldn't believe how kind and caring Lilly was being, apologising to him when he was the one who had failed her.

"And I've been able to finally put the past in the past. Going back made me realise how Oliver and I are so happy here in Cornwall. Cornwall is our home now, not Dorset."

Joel reached out and pulled her into his arms. Kissing the top of her head, he held her tightly to him. "I've missed you, Lilly."

"I've missed you too," she muffled into his shoulder, her arms wrapped around his waist, returning his embrace.

"Do you think you could ever see Pine Trees as your home?" he whispered into her ear.

He felt her pull away from him before looking up at him with her beautiful brown eyes.

"And Oliver of course, and Isla and Milo!" he said with a light heartedness he wasn't actually feeling, as Lilly was yet to reply.

He watched Lilly cast her eyes over the pretty meadow winter paddocks, the gentle stream running alongside them, right down to the summer paddock, where Eliza, Penelope and William were grazing.

"Yes," she replied.

His heart skipped a beat on hearing her answer. That very simple little word shot adrenaline through his veins. As he scooped her up and swung her round in celebration, he heard her whisper in his ear, "Life is to be lived Joel. If there is anything to be learned from what has happened to our sisters, it's that life is short, and we must not take it for granted."

Joel whole-heartedly agreed with her, and in that moment, holding her in his arms, he knew that whatever was ahead of them, whatever their future held, they would face it together.

"Ah, what a relief," jested Joel.

"What is?" queried Lilly.

"That you want Pine Trees to be your home. It's going to make being a horse owner so much easier, you know, living where your horse is."

"Wait, what? What on earth are you talking about?" asked Lilly, confusion etched on her face.

"Kit, of course!" replied Joel, reaching out and stroking the little horse. "Didn't I say? He's for you and Oliver, if you want him?" he said quietly, the laughter now gone from his voice.

"You got me a horse?" Lilly said, her voice full of surprise, but Joel did not detect any sense of unease or disapproval in her tone, encouraging him to be honest with his reply.

"Yes. I'm quite good with horses," he said, the jest returning to his voice. "Or so I'm told, anyway!" And with Lilly giggling along with him, he continued, "And I'm quite good at matching people to the right horses too. And I thought, if Lilly were ever to get a horse, this is the one for her. Plus, he's super safe for Oliver too. So, I considered those good enough reasons to get him for you. I wanted you to enjoy all the fun Eliza and I share together, with your own horse," he admitted.

Lilly released her grip on Joel and wrapped her arms around Kit. "I love him!" And then returning her attention back to Joel, she reached up on her tip toes and planted a kiss on his lips. "Thank you."

Jack

Jack looked over and saw Chloe beaming in delight.

"Did you see that, Dad? I just did rising trot!"

"I did! Well done," he replied with both enthusiasm and pride in his voice.

After his first ride on Issy, and his enjoyable and somewhat therapeutic ride with Joel, he decided riding was something he would like to participate in on a regular basis. And he wanted to learn more about horses in general. Jack was secretly thrilled when Chloe jumped at the chance to accompany him to the local riding school for a riding lesson.

It's not often a teenage girl wants to hang out with her dad on a Saturday afternoon, he mused, and now, three weeks on, their Saturday afternoon at the stables together was becoming routine. He and Chloe had even bought some books on the subject and enjoyed reading them together on Saturday mornings over a leisurely breakfast.

"Ok Jack, your turn now," called out the riding instructor.

Jack looked between the two chestnut ears ahead of him and said, "Walk on Jimmy," and the well-mannered gelding marched off. And with a squeeze of his legs, Jimmy effortlessly transitioned up to a steady trot. Focusing on the smooth rhythm of the horse beneath him, Jack eased himself up, and gently back into the saddle with the beat of Jimmy's trotting pace.

"Brilliant, well done Jack," praised his instructor.

"Well done, Dad!" shouted Chloe.

"Ok, Chloe, you move in behind your dad and continue practising your rising trot together."

Jack felt an overwhelming surge of happiness flow through him as he and Chloe trotted around the sand school. Spending time with his daughter, doing something that brought so much enjoyment to them both, was something every father dreamed of. And right now, he was living that dream. And he had Phoebe to thank. It was Phoebe who had invited him into the world of horses, who had opened up his eyes to the insurmountable pleasure that they offered. And it was Phoebe who showed him the powerful friendship that could be formed between human and horse when there was kindness, gentleness and trust between both parties. He didn't realise what he had been missing until Phoebe let him step into her wonderful world, even if it was for just a short while, and allowed him to see things the way she did. To appreciate all living beings for what they were, and to be content in their company. And Chloe eagerly taking part in his newfound passion was the icing on the cake.

"Ok, guys," said their instructor, "slow them down to walk now. Walk around the school to cool them off then bring them to me and ask them to halt. You have both done brilliantly today."

Jack and Chloe led the horses onto the yard and untacked them. Jack had been clear with the riding stables that he and Chloe did not just want to learn how to ride the horses, but they wanted to learn how to prepare them for riding, and about the care they needed after being ridden, and about how to care for horses in general. The stables had been happy to oblige, and they had a two-hour session each week – an hour for riding, plus half an hour before and after for stable management. Both Jack and Chloe felt that riding was only a small part of what a horse had to offer, and they wanted to learn it all.

Jack and Chloe were busy discussing their lesson whilst they groomed the horses when Jack felt his mobile phone buzz in his pocket. Sliding it out he saw Lilly's number flashing on the screen.

"Chloe, I'm sorry, I have to take this. Can you finish Jimmy for me please?"

"Sure, go ahead," Chloe replied, not even looking up from brushing the under belly of the horse she had been allocated for the day's session.

"Lilly, hi," answered Jack.

"Hi Jack, I wanted to give you that update you asked me about last week," said Lilly.

Jack felt his stomach do a flip as a mixture of anxiety and excitement filtered through him.

"She's still here," Lilly continued. "It's been over a month, and we haven't received one enquiry for her."

"The puppies?" Jack enquired.

"All gone. They were all reserved on the day of the fete and rehomed as soon as they were weaned from their mum," explained Lilly.

Jack closed his eyes and could picture Phoebe, her face full of concern as she looked over from the pile of puppies that she was underneath and expressed her worries of Pixie not finding her forever home. Not finding a family to love her like she deserved to be loved. And Jack remembered the calm-tempered, mild-mannered little dog, who melted under his touch, and snoozed contentedly on his lap. His heart went out to her, passed over for her cute little fluff ball puppies, and he couldn't bear the thought of the kind-hearted little dog being cooped up, all alone, in the rescue centre for a moment longer.

"Jack, are you there?" asked Lilly.

"Yes, sorry! When can I come and collect her?" he asked. Having made his decision, he wanted Pixie to step into her forever home as soon as possible.

"Actually, the reason I called today is that we have a pair of dogs in need of her kennel as soon as possible. Rose and Andrew have gone ff to collect them now. They have been subjected to the most appalling neglect, and they'll need veterinary care as soon as they arrive," she explained, "and when you asked after Pixie last week, well, basically I spoke to Rose, and she said you can collect her today if you want her. She prepared all her paperwork before she left, just in case," finished Lilly.

"We'll be there within the hour," replied Jack, hanging up his phone and slipping it back into his pocket.

"Chloe," he announced, "as soon as we're finished here, we're going shopping!"

"Collar, lead, bed, feed bowl, water bowl, dog food, and toys," announced Chloe. "Do you think that's everything we need?"

"Yes, that's everything on the list that Lilly sent through to us. Now, let's go and collect her!"

Jack watched the excitement ooze out of Chloe as she packed up the boot of the car with all of Pixie's things, double, then triple checking they had everything they needed, before jumping into the passenger seat beside him.

"Come on, Dad! I can't wait to meet her!" replied Chloe.

Jack and Chloe were greeted warmly by Lilly when they arrived at Rosewin.

"Jack, Chloe, it's so lovely to see you both again."

"Hi Lilly, who's this?" asked Chloe, bending down to cuddle the friendly golden Labrador, wagging his tail, waiting expectantly for a stroke.

"That's Milo, my dog. He just loves attention!" laughed Lilly. "He spent the day of the fete with my friend Minnie, which is why you didn't get to meet him then. It was such a busy day that I couldn't look after him properly and fulfil all my fete duties! But usually, he's with me wherever I go. Dogs are wonderfully loyal friends, and Pixie can't wait to meet the family she will bestow her loyalty on.

Shall we go and get her?"

"Oh yes please," replied Chloe.

Lilly and Jack stepped back when Lilly opened Pixie's kennel door, and watched Chloe and Pixie meet for the first time. Pixie wagged her tail with gusto, and when Chloe kneeled down, she placed her paws on Chloe's knees and affectionately licked her nose. "Oh Dad, she's adorable. I love her already!" gushed Chloe. "Can I put this on her now?" asked Chloe, holding up Pixie's brand-new black leather collar.

"Of course, you can," replied Lilly. "She's your dog now, Chloe."

Chloe carefully slipped the collar around Pixie's neck, and the little dog waited patiently for her do up the buckle. Smoothing down Pixie's fur, Chloe announced, "It's a perfect fit, Pixie." Then, clipping the new black lead to her collar, Chloe stood up, and said, "Let's get you out of here!"

Jack watched the little dog walk elegantly beside her new mistress. No pulling, no over excited behaviour, just a calm acceptance that Chloe was going to do right by her. It was as if she knew that Chloe and Jack were to be her new family. She put her trust in Chloe and contentedly agreed to be led by her, knowing that somehow, all would be well.

Once the paperwork had been signed and goodbyes exchanged, Jack, Chloe and Pixie walked out of Rosewin's reception area, eager to start the next phase of their lives as a family of three.

"Do you think I should cancel Meg?" Chloe asked Jack.

"Absolutely not, you've have been helping Meg plan her party for weeks. Think how disappointed she would be if you cancelled one hour before her mum is due to pick you up. I promise you, Pixie and I will be fine," Jack told his daughter. Concern was written all over her face, but he would not let her disappoint Meg.

She was her best friend, and she would be crushed if Chloe didn't go to her party.

"You're right, I can't do that to Meg. I'll go and get ready. Come along Pixie, you can help me decide what to wear." And without hesitation, Pixie jumped off the sofa and merrily skipped along after Chloe.

I've got two of them now! Jack laughed to himself. He was pleased with how quickly Pixie and Chloe had bonded. Living with just her dad, he thought having another female in the house would do her the world of good, even if that female was a dog! He knew that Pixie would be her loyal confidante and a listening ear for all of her secrets, and he felt that Pixie was very much up for the job of supporting Chloe through her teenage years, and beyond. His two girls would look after each other.

Jack stretched his legs out over the sofa, and with Chloe now gone, Pixie graced him with her presence, and snuggled up next to him. Listening to the sounds of Pixie's sleepy snuffles, in the otherwise silent house, Jack finally allowed his thoughts to drift towards Phoebe, and the ache in his heart swelled when he closed his eyes and pictured her in his mind's eye.

Five weeks without so much as a text message. Five weeks without hearing her heart-warming laugh or seeing her smiling face. It felt like a lifetime. And how he ached to wrap his arms around her and hold her close to him, just like he had done all those weeks ago in Rosewin's carpark. He understood her silence. He knew she needed time to heal and time to come to terms with what had happened to her. And he would not pressure her. He would not badger her or bombard her with messages or uninvited arrivals either at the hospital or her home. The flowers and card he sent straight after her accident, plus three other messages reiterating that he was thinking of her and there to support her, were enough.

Now all he could do is wait. He would be there for her whenever she was ready to reach out to him. But it hurt that she had not allowed him to support her, not chosen him to lean on during her time of need. And he desperately hoped that his waiting would not be in vain, that she would reach out to him when she was ready. He couldn't think about the possibility of never seeing or hearing from her again. That was an unbearable thought to him. A future without Phoebe in it - he couldn't possibly imagine such a thing.

Pixie slid off the sofa and nudged his hand gently with her nose, followed by a polite whine, pulled Jack away from his day dreaming.

"Do you need to go out, girl?" he asked her. Another nudge, followed by another whine, confirmed his suspicion.

"Come on, Pixie," Jack said, hauling himself up off the sofa. He clipped her lead on and together they stepped outside for an evening walk. The air was fresh, and the sky cast a warm glow as the deep orange sun descended, as Pixie and Jack strolled around the block, enjoying the quiet evening and just each other for company. With Pixie trotting along beside him, Jack knew he had done the right thing by bringing her into their home. She made their house a home, just by being there, and Jack was so very grateful to Pixie fofilling the void he hadn't even known was there.

Opening his front door, Pixie skipped in, trotted into the sitting room and made herself comfy on the sofa. *She already knows this is home,* he thought, smiling to himself, settling himself next to her. And then his phone beeped. He stared at the screen, and there was her name, right in front of his eyes. The message he had been waiting for. The message that now sent shivers down his spine, since he didn't know if it was to reveal good news or bad news. Living in limbo for the past five weeks had at least given him a glimmer of hope that he might receive good news. But now it was here, he would know for sure, and he wasn't sure if he was ready to read the much-anticipated message.

He looked at Pixie, sitting up next to him, watching him with her kind, gentle eyes. "What do you think, girl?" he asked his new confidante. And he watched her delicately lift her paw and tap his phone.

"You're right, just like ripping off a plaster, best to get it over and done with!" he replied to Pixie. Taking a deep breath, and a quick glance at Pixie for courage, he clicked open message.

Hi Jack, Thank you for the beautiful flowers and card. I'm home from hospital now. I was wondering if you might be free to meet up next weekend? Phoebe x

Lilly

Lilly was pleased to see Oliver wriggling in the back seat with excitement as soon as she pulled into Pine Trees driveway. After the flurry of elation at finally being held in Joel's arms again, and the prospect of moving to Pine Trees and becoming a family, and then there was the giddiness of having their own new horse to contend with too!

Reality had hit home with a wallop when she realised that she would be uprooting Oliver again. He was so happy and settled in their little cosy cottage. His routine, school, and little friendship group were all ticking along effortlessly, and she worried that another move might unsettle him. She had phoned Joel that evening, concerned and panic-stricken about what they should do, reiterating how she wanted to move to Pine Trees, but not to the detriment of Oliver.

Joel's sensible, soothing tone on the other end of the phone had immediately calmed her. They would take it one step at a time, he assured her. They were in no hurry, they both knew what they wanted, and they would get there, no matter how long it took. Oliver would, and should have, as much time as he needed to adjust to the idea of both moving to Pine Trees and Joel becoming part of their family.

Lilly was immediately pacified by Joel's words, and they decided that Oliver should visit Pine Trees, and meet Kit, without any pressure. Lilly had not yet told him that they had acquired a pony. She thought it was only fair for Joel to be there when he found out so they could enjoy his reaction to the exciting news together. Oliver was only told that he was to have a fun day out at Joel's house. And that is exactly what they had organised. One week since meeting Kit herself, it was now Oliver's turn to be introduced to the newest member of their family.

"Joel, Joel," called out Oliver, as soon as Lilly allowed him to unbuckle his seat belt and jump out of the car. Running over to Joel, with Milo hot on his heels, she watched Joel swing the little boy up into the air, much to Oliver's delight.

"Hi Joel," said Lilly, and after Joel carefully placed Oliver safely back on the ground, he reached out his arms to greet her with a hug. They had also discussed that their relationship should not be kept secret from Oliver. Subtle gestures of affection between them would help Oliver understand that they were forging a family unit. *Step by step,* Lilly thought, and she was thrilled by how Oliver greeted Joel with such exuberance. The bond between them was beginning to form, and she knew the more time Oliver spent with Joel, he would come to love him, just as much as she did.

"Your Aunt Lilly and I have someone here who is just desperate to meet you! Would you like to meet him?" Joel asked Oliver.

"Really? Yes Please. Who is it?" replied the little boy, eagerly looking around the yard.

"Come with me," said Joel, and with Lilly following behind, Oliver skipped along beside Joel, over towards the paddock where the four horses were grazing.

"He's a horse!" announced Oliver.

"Yes, he is," replied Lilly. "His name is Kit."

And Lilly watched as Oliver, standing side by side with Joel, tentatively held out his hand to stroke Kit, then promptly burst out laughing when his whiskers tickled his fingers.

"Would you like to ride him?" asked Joel.

Oliver turned to Lilly, and with questioning eyes asked, "Can I?"

Lilly was overjoyed with his enthusiasm, and impressed with his bravery, too. He had never spent much time around horses, let alone ridden one before, and he was far more courageous than she had been the first time Joel suggested she ride Eliza. "Of course you can," she replied.

Kit stood like a statue whilst Oliver bustled around him on the yard, helping to groom him and prepare him for riding. Once tacked up, Joel carefully buckled up the brand-new riding hat he had purchased for him the day before, then lifted him up into the saddle.

Lilly looked on quietly from the side-lines as the little horse helped Joel and Oliver to bond. Oliver hung off every word Joel said about horses, and his childlike sponge of a brain soaked up every single detail.

"Like this?" asked Oliver, taking hold of Kits reins.

"Just like that," replied Joel. "Now, are you ready to go for your first ride?"

"Yes!" squealed Oliver with glee.

Joel took hold of the lunge line and said, "Walk on Kit, you and Oliver are going riding."

Oliver did exactly as Joel told him to do. He sat quietly in the saddle, held the reins gently, and confidently rode around Joel, on the lunge line, in the makeshift schooling paddock. Lilly's heart swelled with pride at seeing him so cool, calm and confident, on board the friendly, trustworthy horse. Joel had been right. Kit was most definitely the perfect horse for both her and Oliver.

"Can we go faster now, Joel?" asked Oliver, grinning from ear to ear.

Lilly returned Joel's questioning look with a brief nod. *He's in safe hands,* she thought. Joel instructed Oliver to squeeze Kit with his legs, and at the same time, Joel voiced, "Trot on Kit."

And Kit smoothly transitioned up into a steady trot, never missing a pace as Oliver learned to balance himself with the bumpy motion of his first trot.

After Joel slowed Kit down to his steady walking pace, he asked, "Fun?"

Giggling wildly, Oliver replied, "Yes! Riding is so much fun, Joel."

"Would you like to leave the paddock and go for a ride around Pine Trees?" asked Joel.

"Oh yes please. Come on Kit, let's go exploring!" replied the very enthusiastic Oliver.

Lilly fell into step beside Oliver, Kit and Joel, and called out, "Walkies!" On hearing that special word, Katie and Milo bounded over from exploring the stables, and zoomed off ahead of them into the long-grassed meadows.

The happy little party ambled through the fields, down towards Pine Trees boundary stream. Joel led Kit to the water for a refreshing drink, whilst the dogs launched themselves into the stream to play. Lilly couldn't help but laugh at their antics, splashing and bounding through the cool water, their tongues lolling and eyes dancing in delight. Lilly cast her eyes all around and soaked up the idyllic scene before her. Entering Pine Trees was like stepping into another world. The grazing horses, fluttering butterflies, buzzing bees, curious bunny rabbits hopping here and there, and the sweet-scented fragranced air from the abundance of wildflowers. The gently cascading river, coupled with the light wind whistling through the pine trees, gave her a sense of peace and tranquillity.

And Joel had asked if she would like to share his exquisite home with him. She could not think of a more perfect place for Oliver to grow up, and for her and Joel to share their lives together. Gratitude swept through her with what Joel was offering both her and Oliver. Her lovely, kind, generous, Joel.

Oliver brought her away from her dreaming when he asked, "Why do you live in a caravan Joel, and not your house?"

"Oliver! Manners please! What have I told you about asking people personal questions," chastised Lilly.

Joel promptly burst out laughing. "It's ok Lilly! Actually, I won't be living in the caravan for much longer." Turning Kit around so Oliver could look back towards the buildings, Joel said, "You see the big one?" He pointed in the direction of the farmhouse.

Oliver nodded. "That's my house, and although it's not quite finished, it's just about ready for me to move into." He moved his finger to point to the other cottage. "Now the other one, that's Phoebe's, she's got another two to three months before hers will be ready to move into. And that one," his finger pointed towards the final barn, "well that one is still just a shell! That one is going to be a holiday cottage eventually. Phoebe and I are going to rent it out so people can come to Pine Trees and enjoy all of this," he said, sweeping his arm across the stables, paddocks, meadows, and awe-inspiring views.

"Wow, how lucky for the people who can come and have a holiday here," replied Oliver.

"You think so?" questioned Lilly.

"Oh yes, they'll get to see the horses every day!" said Oliver.

"Would you like to see Kit every day?" Lilly tentatively asked him.

"Of course I would! I love him," gushed Oliver, leaning down and wrapping his arms around his new friend.

"Maybe, you and Aunt Lilly could come and have a sleep over at my house, one night?" asked Joel.

"Really? Can we Aunt Lilly, please?" replied Oliver.

Lilly slipped her hand into Joel's, and felt his rough, warm fingers link through hers. She felt like she was floating on air. And glancing up at Joel, she knew, underneath his outer calm, reserved exterior, excitement for what lay ahead was also swirling through his veins.

"Yes, I'm sure we can arrange a sleep over at Pine Trees."

Bridget

Nestled in the corner window seat, at one of their favourite Truro cafés, Bridget eagerly awaited Sally's arrival. It had been months since she had last seen her dearest friend. Between Sally's daughter's unexpected arrival home, and Phoebe's tragic accident, they both only had time for their children during their times of need. With Phoebe now out of the woods, and back at home, Bridget finally felt able to leave her for a few hours for a much needed catch up with Sally.

Bridget jumped up with arms outstretched as soon as Sally entered the bustling café. Her friend instantly caught her eye, and in less than a second, weaved her way between the many tables, and into her arms.

"Sally!" exclaimed Bridget.

"Bridget! It's been too long," replied Sally.

Releasing each other from their warm greeting, the two old friends settled into their comfy seats for a long-overdue catch up.

"I've ordered us a cream tea for two," explained Bridget. "I thought we deserved a treat!"

And Bridget watched a broad smile break out on Sally's face when the waitress carried over the plates piled high with freshly baked scones, accompanied by little pots of home-made strawberry jam and clotted cream. Two steaming cups of tea, on elegant saucers decorated with pretty daisies, were placed next to their delicious feast.

"Perfect!" replied Sally.

"How's Phoebe?" was the first question Sally asked.

"Better, well, physically she is. She's terribly scarred, but the burns have healed," replied Bridget as Sally reached out her hand and placed it over her own in comfort.

"I'm so sorry, Bridget, for all that you have been through. What has happened to Phoebe is just heart-breaking. And," she tentatively continued, "how is she in herself?"

"It's been a difficult time," Bridget confessed. "She can't bear to look at herself. Keeps herself covered from top to toe. It doesn't seem to matter how many times I tell her she is still beautiful; she just can't see it. Her confidence has hit rock bottom, and other than me, the only person she sees –" She paused and gave a wry smile. "Well, she's not even a person! But she only sees Penelope."

"At least she leaves the house to go and see her horse, that must be a good thing?" Sally softly replied.

"Yes, you're right, thank goodness for Penelope! And I think Penelope is slowly working her magic. Each time she returns from the yard I see a little sparkle of the old Phoebe. Penelope doesn't treat her any differently to how she did before the accident. How she looks on the outside doesn't make a blind bit of difference to her - Phoebe is still Phoebe in her eyes, and will always be her best friend. I'm hoping all the time she is spending with her will slowly boost her confidence. It's just going to take time. And she told me that she sent Jack a message last week. Apparently, she's agreed to meet him tomorrow," confided Bridget.

"You said Jack was a lovely man," chipped in Sally.

"Oh, he is. Well, I think he is. How do we ever really know?" questioned Bridget, and without waiting for Sally to reply, she ploughed on to share her worries with her friend. "I only hope he doesn't say or do anything to damage what shreds of confidence Penelope and I have painstakingly attempted to restore into Phoebe over the last few weeks," said Bridget, with concern washing over her.

"Our children are all grown up now," said Sally. "All we can do is support them from the side-lines and pick up the pieces when they need us to."

Bridget nodded, taking in her friend's wise words. "Yes, you're absolutely right. What will be will be. And your daughter is still living with you?" asked Bridget, suddenly feeling guilty for monopolising the conversation. Well, truth be told, ever since Phoebe's accident, Sally had been at the other end of the phone for her every single day offering her support and help in any way she could. And Bridget shamefully admitted to herself, *not once did I ask how Sally and her daughter were.*

Sally laughed in reply, "Oh yes, daughter and cat are still residing at Hotel Mum!"

Bridget appreciated the lighter tone that the conversation now took, enabling her to forget her fears of what tomorrow might bring between Phoebe and Jack.

"And I have some gossip," Sally continued. "She's got a date this evening! I promised her I'd pick up a new lipstick before I head home."

"How exciting!" Bridget eagerly replied. "I hope it goes well for her. She deserves to meet someone nice after what the last one did to her. I can't wait to hear all about it."

"And speaking of boyfriends," Sally said with a smile on her face, "how is your dashing Mr Parker?"

Giggling like a pair of schoolgirls, Bridget divulged how wonderful Charles had been since Phoebe's accident, and how his constant support and kindness were what had kept her going during the darkest hours of her recovery.

Bridget heard the Cathedral bells chime four o'clock, "Oh my, is that the time?"

Sally hastily gathered up her handbag, "Bridget, I've had the loveliest afternoon with you," she said, before folding Bridged into her arms for their farewell hug.

"But I must collect the lipstick before the shops shut! She's nervous enough as it is and if I turn up without her war paint, she'll be devastated!"

Bridget nodded knowingly. "This afternoon has just flown by! But then it always does when we get together," admitted Bridget, and both ladies stifled a conspiratorial laugh. "I told Charles that I would message him once we parted, we're going to take Rascal for a walk together," shared Bridget. "And thank you, Sally," she continued with complete sincerity, "thank you for today and for all your kindness over these past weeks. You truly are the most wonderful friend."

After returning her friends embrace, Bridget released her arms and with a wry smile, continued, "Now off you pop for that lipstick! I'll look forward to all the gossip tomorrow!"

After watching her friend walk away, Bridget felt a comforting lightness as she strolled along the cobbled streets of Truro to Charles's office. Time with Sally was exactly what she had needed. Sally was her truest friend, and their friendship was something that she held dearly. They had shared their lives together, through all the ups and downs that life had delivered them. They were always at each other's side, to share the good moments, and to help carry one another's burdens of heartache. *Time spent with a friend, is always time well spent,* Bridget thought as she meandered through the pretty city with a heart full of love and gratitude for having such a wonderful friend.

Bridget was pleasantly surprised to see Charles sitting on the bench just outside his office. His mind was focused on the paperwork he held in his hands, and little Rascal was tucked up next to him on the bench. Her heart fluttered, just like it always did, when she spotted him. Hastening her step, she noticed Rascal jump up and wag his tail on recognising her, disrupting Charles from his work. He looked up and smiled broadly as she approached them.

"Hello, Charles," she said, as she bent down to give him a brief kiss on his cheek. "And hello, Rascal," she said to the little dog who eagerly accepted her affectionate stroke.

"Bridget, hi. Did you have a lovely time with your friend?" asked Charles.

"The best!" replied Bridget, settling herself on the bench next to Charles.

"Rascal and I have had a busy afternoon," announced Charles handing her the papers that he was holding.

Bridget realised that it wasn't work papers at all, but a glossy brochure for a boutique hotel and spa in France. Unable to hide the surprise in her voice, she said, "France! Are you going to France?"

"Actually," replied Charles, as he took her hand in his, and looked directly at her, "Rascal and I were hoping that you would come with us?"

"To France?" Bridget repeated, somewhat flummoxed at this unexpected invitation.

"Yes. Rascal and I have been to the vets to organise his passport. If we go on the ferry from Plymouth, Rascal can come with us. And the travel agent suggested this hotel, not far from Roscoff, which allows dogs to stay, plus they have a wonderful spa and swimming pool."

Bridget was speechless, and just stared blankly back at Charles.

"Not right now, I know Phoebe still needs you to be with her, but when she's ready. When you're ready, I thought it would be nice for you to have a break. I thought it would be nice for someone to look after you for a change." Slowly raising her hand to his lips, he gently placed a kiss on the back of her hand, before continuing, "I'd like to look after you Bridget, if you'll let me?"

Bridget looked into the eyes of the kind, generous man sitting before her, and couldn't believe how lucky she was to have found someone so caring and thoughtful. After all the grief and heartache she had sffered after Jacob, and then Phoebe, she couldn't believe she could feel so happy again.

"Yes," she said to Charles, "I would absolutely love to go to France with you and Rascal once Phoebe is well enough to be left on her own." And with her emotions skyrocketing through her, she reached out her arms and enveloped Charles in a warm embrace. "Thank you," she whispered in his ear, "thank you for everything."

Phoebe

Phoebe closed her eyes and slowly stepped out of her pyjamas.

You can do this, she told herself, *on the count of three, one, two, three,* and she pinged her eyes open to see her naked body staring back at her from her bedroom mirror. She felt her body shudder on reflex at seeing the ugly scars trailing all the way down the left-hand side of her body. She turned to the side, shielding herself from them, and her eyes travelled up and down the smooth, unaffected skin of her right. Holding her breath, she turned the other way, and the full view of her scarred body, hideous markings encasing her neck, all the way down to her knee, glared back at her.

She swallowed the lump forming in her throat and tried to squash the heat of shame prickling through her.

Self-pity is no good for anyone, she told herself firmly. *You've been moping around for weeks, there are people who have suffered much worse than you,* she chastised herself, and looking directly into her own eyes, "Now suck it up, buttercup, you're going riding with friends today, and that's all there is to it," she told herself with a steely determination.

She had not actually planned to go riding with anyone but herself. She had enough worry and concern over her meet up with Jack later in the afternoon, but Mel was a force to be reckoned with! She had contacted her to ask if they could go riding together; she was desperate to meet Penelope and couldn't wait to show off her beloved Percy, and for all of Phoebe's self-pity, it wasn't in her to be mean, and she was perfectly capable of riding now. Although she lacked strength in her left side from the accident, Penelope seemed to sense she needed to take care of her mistress, and she did. The few rides she had been on, Penelope behaved perfectly, not a hoof out of place, and proved that she could be trusted, even with Phoebe's weakened left-hand side. And Phoebe could not think of an excuse not to ride. And then guilflooded her when she knew how upset Ellen would be if she were to ride with a complete stranger instead of her! So somehow it had been agreed that Mel would hack Percy over to Pine Trees, and together they would hack up to the moors and meet Ellen and Jupiter, and Phoebe would not let her friends down. She had always been thoughtful and loyal to her friends. *And just because I look like this,* she thought, *does not give me an excuse to behave rudely.*

She and her mother had carefully chosen her outfit for riding the day before. Her favourite navy-blue jodhpurs paired with a long-sleeved sky-blue coloured shirt that enabled her to button up the cuffs to stop them from rising and showing off any more of her scarred skin than necessary, and the top button did up high on her neck. High enough to hide the scars yet lose enough not to cause her discomfort. And new gloves. They had been a gift from Joel, and she smiled as she slipped her hands inside the beautiful soft, navy blue leather riding gloves.

Phoebe was just lifting Penelope's saddle onto her back when she heard the sound of a horse clip clopping towards her. Turning round she was greeted with a beaming Mel, proudly riding her adorable Häflinger, Percy.

"Phoebe!" she called out in friendly greeting, "meet Percy. Percy, this is our new friend Phoebe."

Phoebe couldn't help but laugh at Mel's quirky little ways. "Hi Mel, and it's lovely to meet you, Percy," she replied. "This is Penelope."

"She's a real beauty," gushed Mel, before Phebe heard her whisper, "Don't you worry Percy, you're my best boy," into Percy's golden ear.

Smiling to herself, she finished tightening Penelope's girth, placed her foot in the stirrup and climbed aboard her horse.

Penelope and Phoebe plodded alongside Mel and Percy, as Mel chatted away, ten to the dozen, about her new life since moving to her boyfriend's family farm.

You just can't help but like her, thought Phoebe. Mel oozed bubbly loveliness, and everyone and everything in her little world was idyllic. Phoebe remembered how her world used to be just like Mel's, and how she only ever saw the goodness in people and the beautiful world and wonderful earthly creatures that she shared with it. Being with Mel was helping her to remember how lucky she was to be alive, and to enjoy, in that very moment, the perfect countryside view that she could see through two little brown ears, straight ahead of her. Her mind began to clear as she listened to the steady beat of Penelope's shoes on the tarmac of the country lane, and with Mel merrily announcing each and every pretty flower, grazing animal, or magnificent, ancient tree that they came across, Phoebe felt a little bit of her old self reigniting within her.

"Oh wow!" squealed Mel, when they stepped out of the overgrown track and set foot on the wide-open moors. "What a view!"

Phoebe returned her smile, before replying, "Beautiful, isn't it? Ellen and I ride here all the time. Come on, follow me, she should pop out of the other overgrown entrance just up here."

And right on cue, Phoebe heard Ellen's voice. "Hello, Phoebe, you guys there?"

Jupiter's regal head appeared around the gateway, and then there she was, her funny, kind friend, who she had put off seeing for so long. Right in that moment, Phoebe couldn't for the life of her think why. Ellen's cheerful smile greeted her, just like always, and Penelope and Jupiter nickered their own horsey greeting.

It has been too long, thought Phoebe, breathing in the fresh countryside air coupled with the sweet smell of the horses, and listening to the gentle chatter of Mel and Ellen introducing themselves. Phoebe realised that shutting herself away had not been productive at all. Here, right now, with her friends and the horses, was the best she had felt since the accident.

"Swish swoo!" remarked Ellen. "Penelope is looking very posh in her new saddle pad!"

Grinning broadly, Phoebe replied, "I know, she's now the poshest pony in the whole of Cornwall! We love it, don't we Pen. Thank you, Ellen."

Phoebe, her confidence growing in the company of her friends, turned to them, and with a grin, said, "Who's up for a race!" And before the others had chance to reply, she squeezed her legs and Penelope shot off like a rocket.

Phoebe could hear her friends laughing behind her, and the thunder of Jupiter's and Percy's hooves as they picked up pace to catch up with her and Penelope. Penelope continued to build up speed, and when they reached the slightly uphill stretch of moors, she gave one more teeny squeeze with her legs, and they hit fifth gear. Penelope hurtled across the moors and, giving her a loose rein, Phoebe just held on for the ride.

"Ok, ok, you win!" said Ellen, breathless from their long run.

Slowing their horses down, Ellen and Mel rode up beside Phoebe. "Blimey you guys can ride!" said Mel. "That was so much fun."

"Wait until we take you through the woods," said Ellen. "There are some great canter tracks and plenty of logs to jump."

"I can't wait!" replied Mel.

"We'll take you to the woods next week," announced Phoebe, determined that from now on, she would do her best to get back to normal, and riding every week with her friends was very much normal.

The three friends slipped through the narrow gateway that brought them back onto the quiet Cornish country lanes and they continued planning their next adventurous ride until they met the fork in the road.

"Well, this is me," said Ellen. "It was lovely to meet you, Mel." Then she leaned forward to embrace Phoebe in an awkward hug from horseback. "And it has been so good to see you Phoebe, roll on next week!"

Phoebe watched her friend clip clop along the lane, back to Hollybrook stables, excitement fluttering within her for their next ride together.

"We go this way," she told Mel, directing Penelope down the lane headed for Pine Trees.

"Thank you for today," said Mel, when Pine Trees came into sight. "I've had the most wonderful time."

Phoebe looked at her new friend, and with her new positive outlook she thought that if it hadn't been for her accident, she would never have met her. *If it wasn't for her, I wouldn't be alive! Mel is most definitely the silver lining from my accident.*

"You are most welcome. And Mel, I can't thank you enough for what you did. Dragging me out of a burning car takes courage, and you have that in spades! You saved my life."

Mel returned her gaze and smiled shyly. "Anyone would have done it!" she said, light-heartedly shrugging off Phoebe's heartfelt comment. "Happy to have helped," she continued, resuming her usual bubbly tone.

As they reached Pine Tree's entrance, Phoebe said, "Same time next week?"

"Percy and I will be here with bells on!" she replied, before pushing Percy into a brisk trot for the final leg of their journey home.

Phoebe let go of Penelope's reins and let her guide herself down the drive and home to the yard. Idly dreaming about next week's ride, and the fun it would entail, Phoebe jolted back into reality when she saw Jack's car parked next to hers in front of the yard. She glanced at her watch.

Good grief, I was supposed to meet him at home half an hour ago. Time had somehow seemed inconsequential when she was with her friends. Everything had been forgotten and she had been living in the moment, enjoying every single second of laughing, playing, and gossiping, not to mention racing on the moors!

But she was mortified at having forgotten her meeting with Jack, and she rapidly tried to regain her composure before he spotted her. She saw him first - he had his back to her as he stood by the paddock gateway, giving scratches to the ever-attention-seeking William, and he was not alone. A slim girl was standing next to him, also showering William in affection.

That must be Chloe, thought Phoebe, as she gently squeezed the reins and asked Penelope to halt.

"Hi Jack," she called out, still sitting on Penelope, hoping that staying on board would help her remain in her comfort zone as her addled brain tried desperately to grapple with the situation unfolding before her, and the fact that even after all this time, her heart skipped a beat on seeing him and she felt the familiar zing shoot through her body.

"I hope you don't mind us meeting you at the yard," stammered Jack, and Phoebe realised that he was just as nervous as she was. "Your mum told us you had gone riding with friends, and suggested we meet you here instead of at home."

"Of course, it's fine. I'm so sorry I'm late, I completely lost track of time," blurted out Phoebe, trying to fill the somewhat awkward silence. "And you must be Chloe?"

"Yes, hi Phoebe, it's so lovely to finally meet you," the girl replied. "Can I meet your horse?"

Effortlessly dismounting from Penelope, Phoebe gestured for Chloe to come closer. "You can pet her if you like?" And Phoebe watched a smile creep onto the girls face at being invited over to touch the beautiful Penelope.

"She's stunning," murmured Chloe, gently stroking Penelope's nose.

After a few moments of petting Penelope, Chloe stepped back from the horse. "I guess you guys have lots to talk about," she announced astutely, then stepping towards Phoebe, she reached out and gave her a brief hug, taking her quite by surprise, before saying, "It really is wonderful to meet you." Then she turned to her dad and said, "Can I take Pixie for a walk now please?"

"Yes, but don't go too far," replied Jack. And Phoebe watched her skip off to the car, open the door, and out jumped Pixie. *The* Pixie. Phoebe stared open-mouthed on seeing the little dog gleefully dancing around Chloe before trotting along at her heels as she headed off towards the winter meadows.

"You adopted Pixie?" questioned Phoebe, gesturing for Jack to follow her so she could untack Penelope and turn her out into the paddock with her friends.

"Yes, Lilly kept me in the loop, and after all of her puppies had been adopted, I couldn't bear the thought of her being all alone in the kennels, so she came home with us. She's Chloe's dog really. When Chloe is home, she never leaves her side, but I seem to be acceptable company when Chloe isn't around," he said wryly.

"I'm so pleased for Pixie," Phoebe said, and for the first time she looked up and met his eyes. The sparkling green eyes she had first seen when he came to her rescue all those months ago. It felt like another lifetime. And she saw the pain in his eyes, the pain that she had caused for blocking him from her life. Being so close to him brought back all the memories, and all those feelings she had for him before chaos had bulldozed its way into her life.

He took a step towards her, and she didn't flinch. She couldn't move. All of her buried emotions suddenly unleashed within her, swarming her body and mind. She felt her heart thumping against her chest when he took another step towards her. He was close enough to reach out his hand and stroke Penelope's nose.

"Jack," she stammered "I'm so sorry."

"Don't be," he replied, his voice steady and calm. "You have nothing to apologise for."

Her overwhelming emotionsfinally got the better of her and she could feel tears slowly slipping down her cheeks. Jack's eyes didn't leave hers when he finally covered the ground between them and tenderly placed his hands on her tear-stained cheeks before leaning forward and softly brushing his lips against hers. Pulling away, she felt her breath quicken as he slowly slid his fingers down to her shirt buttons. Carefully undoing the top two buttons, he gently traced his finger down her scarred neck and along her discoloured collar bone. Phoebe froze on feeling his touch and panic soared through her with him finally seeing her scars.

Finally, dropping his gaze, Jack wrapped her up in his arms and held her close to him. Whispering in her ear, he said, "I've missed you Phoebe."

Phoebe's roller coaster of emotions finally settled as soon as she rested her head on his shoulder and relaxed into his arms. "I've missed you too, so very much Jack."

She was sandwiched between Penelope and Jack now, with his arms still holding her tightly.

She felt his body pressing against her, as he softly asked, "Phoebe, will you marry me?"

Printed in Great Britain
by Amazon

20110531R00109